KU-066-510

LAST RECKONING FOR THE PRESIDIO KID

A stagecoach robbery and a train explosion announce the sudden return of the elusive Presidio Kid. Little is known about the Kid, or what triggered these events. In an isolated mountain cabin, Clugh Bendix nurses a leg wound, vowing to discover who shot him. He must travel to the volatile Texas borderlands, to the heart of the mystery of the Presidio Kid. The mystery becomes a battle and he must rely on his wits and his guns to survive.

LEICESTER CITY LIBRARIES	
68404032361 687	
ULVERSCROFT	3 1 AUG 2012
	8·99

EMMETT STONE

LAST RECKONING FOR THE PRESIDIO KID

Complete and Unabridged

LINFORD
Leicester

First published in Great Britain in 2011 by
Robert Hale Limited
London

First Linford Edition
published 2012
by arrangement with
Robert Hale Limited
London

The moral right of the author has been asserted

Copyright © 2010 by Emmett Stone
All rights reserved

British Library CIP Data

Stone, Emmett.
   Last reckoning for the Presidio Kid.- -
(Linford western library)
1. Western stories.
2. Large type books.
I. Title II. Series
823.9'2–dc23

   ISBN 978–1–4448–1241–1

Published by
F. A. Thorpe (Publishing)
Anstey, Leicestershire

Set by Words & Graphics Ltd.
Anstey, Leicestershire
Printed and bound in Great Britain by
T. J. International Ltd., Padstow, Cornwall

This book is printed on acid-free paper

1

After the shooting Bendix must have passed out. When he came round he was lying in the snow which had partially covered him. The snowstorm had ceased but the skies were still heavy. For a few moments he felt nothing, then the pain in his leg started up and it was remorseless. Groaning, he tried to move but the pain rolled over him like an avalanche and he lapsed once more into unconsciousness.

When he came round the second time night had fallen and a snowstorm was howling across the mountainside. He was chilled to the bone, but the pain in his leg had receded. In fact he could feel nothing of his lower limbs and he realized that he was on the way to freezing to death. Something warm and fuzzy was beginning to wrap itself around his consciousness. It was tempting to give way to it but he had enough awareness remaining to know that if he was to have any chance of survival he must gather himself together and reach down into whatever last reserve of energy he might possess.

Gritting his teeth, he began to pull himself towards the cabin. He still had some control over his upper body. Maybe it was the strength he had acquired in his shoulders from all that recent hard work chopping wood, climbing the mountain, setting traps and fishing the streams. Whatever it was, he needed it now to haul himself along, clutching at the earth, seeking a purchase for his fingernails. He felt a stab of pain in his left foot and began to try and push with it. It gave him an extra hold and slowly, slowly he inched his way along the ground till with a final despairing effort he heaved himself over the doorsill of the cabin where he lay immobile as snow blew in gusts though the open door.

Night descended. Fitfully he slept

but only to be awakened each time by the crashing pain in his right knee. He had no way of knowing how much damage the bullet had caused but the fact that he could move at all gave him courage that the leg was not completely smashed. As it was he had lost a lot of blood and he knew he needed to stop the flow. There was a bottle of whiskey on the floor of the cabin. He had been pouring himself a drink when he first heard the sound of the intruder and he had placed it beside the rocking-chair. Coming out of another troubled interim of sleep, he turned his head to look for the bottle. The night was bright and windy. He could see the bottle lying in a broad swath of moonlight and, gritting his teeth against the pain, he managed to crawl the few yards till he could reach it.

Pushing with his left knee, he succeeded in propping himself up against a leg of the table. He reached down, slashed his trousers with his Bowie knife and took hold of the whiskey bottle. He poured part of its contents over the wound, flinching as he did so. Looking down, he was relieved to see that his leg appeared to be intact. There was no bone protruding and he guessed the bullet had somehow ricocheted from his knee. It was still badly damaged. He undid his kerchief, made a tourniquet and fastened it as tightly as he could around his upper leg. Then he put the bottle of whiskey in his mouth and took a deep draught. By the time he had finished the bottle the pain had subsided and he felt a whole lot better.

The days that followed were very bad. At first he was unable to move at all but thirst finally drove him to make the effort needed. Snow had gathered in a pile just inside the doorway and he used it to drink and to bathe his wound. He found an old buffalo robe and covered himself with it. The weather was freezing but at the same time the biting cold probably helped to save his leg from becoming gangrenous and kept the wound clean. He had a supply of whiskey but he was wise enough to use it sensibly. He survived on strips of jerky and, when he was able to move with slightly less pain, on water from a trough outside. He would have to break the frozen surface. All the time he could only move in a slow and painful crawl, but he knew he must soon begin to try and place some weight upon the injured leg.

He started to try and lift and straighten the damaged limb. Struggling to get on a chair, he attempted to move the knee, first to the right, then to the left and then to bend it. The pain was excruciating and the knee was very swollen and tight. All down the back of the leg the bruising was severe. He pulled himself upright using his good leg, then attempted to straighten as well as bend the damaged knee.

There were trees surrounding the cabin and he considered how he might go about making himself a crutch from a branch. In the end he used his rifle.

Very slowly at first but then more quickly he began to regain the use of his right knee. He soon realized, however, that while he might achieve a sufficient degree of mobility to be able to get about once more, it would take weeks before the knee would regain anything like a semblance of its old flexibility; it would never function in the same way again. He would always walk with something of a limp. But that wasn't so bad. At least he would be able to move with relative freedom. It could all have been a lot worse.

The morning came when he was able to hobble down the path which led away from the cabin. The weather had turned milder, making for treacherous conditions under foot. The snow lay thick in the woods and on the mountainside but had turned to a slippery tainted slush all around. Water dripped from the eaves. Taking it slow and using the rifle as a crutch, he made his way along the track, moving downhill, till he could see the remains of his assailant lying in the wet grass. It wasn't a pretty sight. Every instinct told him to ignore the corpse, but he had to see whether he could find any information about who the man was or why he had attempted to kill him. He covered his mouth with a bandanna and, holding his head away, he felt inside the man's pockets. There was nothing to be found other than a slim wallet, a pack of Bull Durham and a card. He checked carefully a second time to make sure he had not missed anything. Then he took the man's gunbelt and rifle, which were lying at a little distance, and kicked the body over the side of a precipice. After he had done that he fastened the gunbelt around his waist and picked up the rifle. Carrying it made walking even more difficult, but slowly and awkwardly he made his way back to the cabin.

When he got there he threw the man's weapons on to a bunk, first taking out one of the revolvers to examine it. It was a Smith & Wesson of a type with which he was not familiar. It was .44 calibre rather than the usual .32 or .22, and it was heavier than the ones he was accustomed to. It seemed to be a more than capable man-stopper. He guessed it was new on the market. Whoever his assailant was, he came well equipped. Sitting at the table, his damaged right leg held stiffly at an angle, he next looked at the card. It read:

Bolton Moss
Delivery Guaranteed

The card was embossed with the figure of an eagle with a salmon in its claws.

'Bounty Hunter,' Bendix muttered to himself. 'Fancy card don't mean nothin'.'

He had a low opinion of the breed, no matter how they duded it up, but it immediately started him thinking. There was no price on his head. So that meant this Bolton Moss was being paid by someone to track him down and kill him, or else it was a case of mistaken identity. Over the years he had made enemies but he couldn't think of anyone who would resort to that kind of measure. His brow wrinkled in thought, he turned to the wallet and emptied its contents on the table. There wasn't much: some dollar bills, a used railroad ticket, a hotel bill from the Pearl Hotel, Driftwood, Wyoming Territory. It seemed like the man had come West on the Union Pacific, stayed two nights at the Pearl, and then ridden up into the mountains. He had known where to find Bendix. Thinking over his two theories, Bendix came to the conclusion that it was a case of mistaken identity. It was Ed Gilpin whom Bolton Moss had been looking for.

Gilpin was the man who had built the cabin and lived in it for years. Bendix had met him a long time before, when they were both riding for an outfit called the Crazy E. They became friends and rode together till Bendix decided to try his luck prospecting.

Later he heard that things hadn't gone so well for Gilpin and that he had dropped out of sight. In the course of his travels Bendix heard some talk and then decided to find what had become of his old friend.

He found him in the cabin high in the mountains. He had built it himself and had been living there in isolation. When Bendix discovered him, Gilpin was already far gone in the illness which took his life a few weeks later. Bendix did what he could to look after him and make him comfortable and when he died he had buried him in a tiny clearing in the woods behind the shack.

And now it seemed that someone was out to get Gilpin. But what could it have been about? Gilpin was a good man. He was not the type to have enemies who would go to such lengths to kill him. Whatever had happened in the past, it must have been some considerable time ago. It was nearly two years since Bendix had erected the wooden cross in the clearing. He had only returned to the cabin recently because he was at a loose end and not sure what to do next. There was a woman involved and the cabin had seemed a natural choice to stay and lick his wounds.

A stab of pain jarred his leg. Now he was literally carrying a wound and he had a new purpose. He would find out what this business was all about. Maybe it wasn't really his concern, but he had a personal stake in it now. More than that: Gilpin had been his friend. He owed it to his memory.

Next morning he stood by the grave of his old comrade. The sky was cloudy and a thin rain spread across the mountainside like mist.

'Whatever this is about,' he said, 'I'll settle it. Lie easy.'

He turned away and climbed painfully into leather. It wasn't an easy matter but only a couple of weeks ago it would have been impossible. He was riding a big steeldust. It was getting a bit old, like Bendix himself, but it was sure-footed and made light work of the difficult trail down the mountain. Now that the weather had broken the way was easier, but great slabs of ice and melting snow remained and further down the mountain the path was so narrow that in places Bendix's foot hung out over space. Gilpin had chosen his hideout well. Towards the bottom of the mountain the trail was strewn with boulders and rock debris, overgrown with low brush and some stunted trees. Beyond that the land was ridged and broken with few trails, but Bendix was familiar with it. In the diffused morning light with a haze of rain sweeping across it like a curtain it had a strange, ethereal look. He let the horse go at its own steady pace. There was some way to go before he reached Driftwood.

Driftwood was a township like many others. The wide main street was flanked by false-fronted frame buildings comprising the usual businesses; a general store, a barber shop, several saloons, a bank, an eating-house. About two thirds of the way down there was a central square with some shade trees and a clapboard church with a squat tower and opposite to it, as if by way of contrast, the marshal's office and jailhouse.

After leaving his horse at the livery stables, Bendix made his way to the Pearl Hotel. It was easy to find, being the largest building in town. Checking in for the night, he asked if he might look at the register. The clerk was a bored youth. He shrugged his shoulders to indicate he had no objection to Bendix's request. Bendix thumbed through the register until he came upon the name of Bolton Moss. He hadn't expected to find it, assuming that the bounty hunter would have used a false name. The man had signed himself with a fine flourish. Bendix was closing the register when he asked the desk clerk if he remembered anything about him. The youth shook his head and Bendix turned to go up the stairs.

'Hold on a moment,' the clerk said.

'Yeah?' Bendix said.

The youth had a frown on his features as if he was trying to remember something. Bendix produced a couple of dollar bills.

'Now that you mention it,' the youth continued, 'there was something. He was carryin' a picture of a man. Asked me if I'd ever seen him in town. We get a sprinklin' of people passin' through, headed for the mountains.'

'Had you seen the man before?' Bendix enquired.

'Nope. Reckon it was just a long shot.'

'Can you remember what the man on the picture looked like?'

'Sorry. I only took one look. It was just a face like any other.'

'What sort of a picture was it? A photograph?'

'Seemed like it was torn off somethin'.'

Bendix nodded and went on up the stairs. His room was on the second floor. There was a bed, a wardrobe and

14

a chair but not much else. It was like a lot of rooms he had been in: bare and functional. Maybe some day there would be something better. He was happier sleeping beneath the stars. He threw himself down on the bed and began to think about what the desk clerk had told him. Moss had certainly been here and he had been looking for someone; the man in the picture. Where had the likeness come from? The clerk had said it appeared to be torn from something. Bendix suddenly sat up. Could it have been torn from a Wanted poster? A wanted man was the normal target for a bounty hunter. Could his friend Gilpin have had a price on his head? At first he was inclined to dismiss the idea, but then he began to have second thoughts. What did he really know about Gilpin? Sure, they had ridden together, but cowboys were a very private breed. They liked to keep themselves to themselves. What might have happened to Gilpin after he split from him? The only thing he knew for certain was that Gilpin had sought the isolation of his mountain hideout. What reason might lie behind his choice? The more Bendix thought about it, the more reasonable the hypothesis became. There was one way to find out. He would pay a visit to the marshal and ask if there were any old wanted dodgers out on Ed Gilpin.

Early the next morning he made his way over to the marshal's office. The marshal was a sharp-featured man in his late thirties. He looked up at Bendix with steely grey eyes.

'Stranger in town?' he drawled.

'Yeah. Just passin' through.'

The marshal looked Bendix up and down. 'Somethin' wrong with that right leg?' he asked.

Bendix had not been aware that he was carrying it awkwardly. He had only taken a few steps into the marshal's office.

'Old range accident,' he replied.

The marshal continued to regard him fixedly. 'We get a few visitors since the spur line link,' the marshal said, 'but I don't figure you come on the train.'

'Been ridin',' Bendix replied.

The marshal's steady gaze relaxed. He swung round on his chair.

'I guess you got some business with me,' he said. 'Make sure it don't turn out the other way round. What can I do for you?'

Bendix liked the man. The night he had spent in the hotel had been quiet. There had been little to disturb him. He guessed the marshal ran a tight town.

'My name is Bendix,' he said. 'Clugh Bendix. Without goin' into a lot of details, I have an interest in a man called Gilpin, Ed Gilpin. He died some time ago. I have some reason to believe that when he died he may have been a wanted man.' He paused. The marshal was looking at him intently again.

'I don't know how long you keep old Wanted posters. I was wonderin' if you might have anythin' on him.'

The marshal did not immediately

reply. He seemed to be considering Bendix's words. After a time he reached into a drawer and produced a folded sheet of paper.

'Gilpin,' he said. 'Would this be him?' He sat up and tossed the parchment to Bendix. It was crinkled and discoloured. Bendix opened it out. Looking up at him from the page was the face of his old friend, looking a lot younger than he remembered him last. He quickly glanced down at the writing.

$250 reward. For the arrest and conviction of Edward Gilpin. Wanted for Robbery and Murder. Dead or Alive.

Before he had finished reading the poster, the marshal's voice interrupted him.

'Now it's a funny thing,' he said. 'That poster has been lyin' about for at least three years. I got a whole collection just like it. I don't know who any of 'em are or where they are.

Nobody ever showed no interest and I doubt if I ever looked at any one of 'em again after the first time. Then suddenly I get two people in as many weeks askin' questions about the same *hombre*.'

Bendix looked up. 'Two people?' he said.

'So far.'

Bendix thought quickly. 'This other person. Did he give a name?'

'Sure did.'

There was a pause. 'Would you mind sayin' what it was?'

The hint of a smile spread across the marshal's countenance. 'Why don't you tell me,' he said.

Bendix nodded. 'OK. If he was who I think he was, his name was Moss, Bolton Moss.' The marshal continued to look at Bendix for a moment before replying.

'Yeah. That was the name. And now I think it might be an idea if you told me just how you really came by that limp.'

Bendix could see that the marshal had sized him up pretty accurately. In a few words he told him about what had happened at the cabin.

'Never did like bounty hunters,' the marshal said when he had finished. He rose to his feet and came round the corner of the table to stand beside Bendix.

'Name's Jennings,' he said. 'Will Jennings. I was just about to take a break when you came through the door. Why not join me in a mug of coffee? I can surely recommend the Rendezvous restaurant.'

After locking the door of the office behind them the marshal guided Bendix across the square and a short way along the main street to the eating-house. Inside there were a few tables covered in white linen cloths. A sideboard with plates and glasses stood against one wall and behind a counter a door led into the kitchen. The place was quiet and they seated themselves beside a window. A waitress brought them coffee.

'I guess you're wonderin' what your

friend Gilpin got himself involved in?' the marshal said.

'Yeah. The poster said he was wanted for robbery and murder.'

'It was some time ago,' the marshal replied. 'I don't remember the details. I only remember it at all because I'd only recently taken over as town marshal. Besides, most of it happened somewhere else. As I recall, there were a series of railroad hold-ups. They got away with a lot of loot. Used to bring the train to a halt by ripping up the line or placing somethin' in the way. Used dynamite a lot of the time to blow up the safe. They struck lucky too often for them not to have had inside information. The leader of the gang was an *hombre* went by the name of the Presidio Kid.'

'I remember readin' somethin' about it,' Bendix replied. 'I still can't quite figure how Gilpin would have got involved in somethin' like that.'

The marshal shrugged his shoulders. 'Who knows?' he said. 'Seems there was about dozen of 'em altogether, includin' the Presidio Kid. There were pretty good descriptions of most of 'em — they didn't seem to take a lot of effort to disguise themselves. So far as I know, though, none of 'em was ever caught. The railroad company employed extra guards and the last time the gang attacked they were taken by surprise. A couple of them got wounded. After that things quieted down. They seemed to just melt away. Maybe they decided to retire on what they'd stolen. There was more than enough for them to make a pretty good life for themselves.

'You say there were good descriptions of 'em?'

The marshal shrugged. 'Wouldn't take much for a man to disguise himself. It's a big country. Nobody asks too many questions.'

'When did you say the last of these train robberies took place?' Bendix asked.

'Couple of years ago.'

The marshal had been looking out of the window. Now he turned back to Bendix. 'I guess that about clears things up as far as you're concerned,' he said. Bendix poured himself another mug of the thick black coffee. 'In a way,' he replied. 'But there's somethin' about all this that doesn't seem to fit. You don't ride with a man and not know somethin' about him. I still can't see Gilpin bein' involved with this Presidio Kid or his gang.'

'Things happen to a man. Circumstances change. There's no denyin' the evidence of that Wanted dodger.'

'Maybe,' Bendix replied.

The marshal was leaning back in his chair and looking out of the window again. Just coming into view along the street was a bunch of three riders. His flinty eyes watched them as they approached the restaurant, then passed by in a cloud of dust.

'What is it?' Bendix asked.

'Probably nothin'. Just some riders.'

The marshal got to his feet and walked out of the door. Leaning on a post, he watched the horsemen as they carried on down the street and then dismounted outside the Yellow Duster saloon. After tying their horses to the hitch-rack they climbed the boardwalk and entered through the batwing doors. The marshal turned and came back inside. Bendix poured the last of the coffee.

'Well,' the marshal said to Bendix, 'I guess I'll leave you to it. Call in and see me before you leave town.'

'Thanks for the help,' Bendix said.

He watched through the net curtains as the marshal made his way down the street. Instead of carrying on in the direction of the town square he crossed the strip and walked up to the horses tied outside the saloon. He spent a few moments looking at the mounts of the three men he had watched as they rode into town, then he strode through the saloon doors. When Bendix called the waitress he found that the marshal had already paid.

Marshal Jennings examined the horses to see if they carried any brand markings. Two of them were marked with a Rocking-Chair, the other was unbranded. Bending down to examine the markings more closely, he thought he could detect possible signs of alteration but he couldn't be sure. It would be easy enough, he reflected, to change, say, an Eleven Half-Circle to a Rocking-Chair. Maybe he was being too canny, but there was something about the three riders that aroused his suspicions. They didn't look like regular cowpokes.

He stepped on to the boardwalk, pushed aside the batwings and strode into the saloon. The three riders were standing together at the bar. They had their backs to him but he could see that they were watching his approach reflected in the mirror behind the counter. Other eyes were on him and a couple of the customers slipped out through the batwings. The bartender looked up at his approach.

'What can I get you, Marshal?' he said.

Jennings shook his head. 'Just a courtesy call,' he replied. 'Maybe later.' He turned to the nearest of the riders. 'You gentlemen aimin' to stay or just passin' through?'

There was no response. The man's eyes met the marshal's in the bar-room mirror.

'Either way,' Jennings continued, 'you seem to have missed the sign on the way into town.'

The man's head turned slowly. 'Yeah? What sign was that?'

'The one sayin' to check in your guns with the marshal. That's me.' The man looked at his companions. A slow grin spread across his features.

'Anybody notice a sign?' he asked.

The others looked thoughtful. One of them dragged a hand across his stubbled blue chin.

'Nope,' he said after a moment's pause. 'Can't say as I did.'

The one next to the marshal turned

to him. 'Nobody saw no sign. Maybe it just got blowed over.'

'Well, makes no difference either way. Now I'm here in person, I'll just ask you to unbuckle your gunbelts and hand in your weapons right now.'

The man raised his glass and swallowed what was left of his whiskey. Jennings was suddenly aware of how quiet the saloon had become. The chatter of voices had died away. The piano player sat with his hands on his knees. Jennings caught the eye of the bartender. He was inching away from the centre of the bar. The man refilled his glass and took another swallow.

'Sorry,' he said. 'Can't oblige.'

'I ain't askin' again, but I'll give you two choices. Either hand over the artillery or mount up right now and get out of town. And make sure you don't come back again.'

'We don't like takin' orders,' the man said.

'I'm givin' you ten seconds to make up your mind,' Jennings replied.

The man looked towards the others. Almost imperceptibly they had begun to fan out away from the bar. The other customers had moved as far away as they could. Jennings had known from the start of the conversation what the outcome would be. He was ready and waiting for one of them to make the first move.

'OK,' the man next to him said. 'Guess we've about finished anyway.'

He made to move away from the bar and in the same instant that his hand fell towards his gun, Jennings's Navy Colt was already in his hand and spitting lead. The man's grin transformed into a look of disbelief as he slid to the floor. The other two had been taken by surprise at the swiftness of Jennings's draw and it gave him the fraction of time he needed to turn and fire. The bullet caught the man on the right in the shoulder and he reeled backwards. A bullet from the third man went whining past Jennings's ear and the mirror splintered into a thousand pieces.

Jennings dived for the floor as another bullet thudded into the wall. As he rolled over he fired again, but the man flung himself behind a table. Jennings was in an exposed position and it wasn't looking good, when suddenly the batwing doors flew apart and Bendix burst into the room, the Smith & Wesson in his hand. Sizing up the situation in a moment, he fired at the man partly concealed behind the table. The bullet crashed into the wood and splinters flew into the man's face. Before he could react another bullet caught him in the chest and he fell forward. The other man was fanning the hammer of his gun as he made a desperate attempt to reach a side door but he got no further as lead from both Jennings and Bendix lifted him from his feet and sent him clattering to the floor. The noise of firing had been deafening. Now a deep silence descended on the smoke-filled room. Bendix looked towards the figure of the marshal still sprawled on the floor.

'You OK, Jennings?' he called.

'Sure. Don't know what would have happened if you hadn't shown up.' Jennings got to his feet. Together, he and Bendix examined the bodies of the gunmen. All three of them were dead. Slowly the saloon began to return to life. People emerged from where they had attempted to find shelter. A ripple of conversation started up. From behind the bar the swamper appeared with a bucket and a mop.

'Somebody get the undertaker,' Jennings said.

Together he and Bendix made for the batwings. As they emerged on to the boardwalk the piano player began to strike up a slow tune.

They made their way back to the marshal's office. When they got there Jennings produced a bottle of bourbon and poured drinks.

'Well,' he said, 'it's my guess that you've got the Presidio Kid on your trail now.'

'What do you mean?' Bendix replied.

'Seems to me it's no coincidence that first Moss turns up out of the blue and now those three owlhoots.'

'I'm not sure I follow.'

'I reckon somethin's happened to resurrect a few old scores. Somebody, maybe Moss, found out where Gilpin had been hidin' out. Moss set out to claim the bounty. It's my opinion that word got out. The Presidio Kid and his gang are followin' on close behind Moss. Maybe some of them are at the cabin right now.'

'Even if you're right about Gilpin's cover bein' blown, why would they do that?'

The marshal shrugged. 'Who knows? Why did Gilpin drop out? Maybe he let them down in some way, maybe he knew somethin'. Those three are just the first arrivals. Once the Presidio Kid and his gang got to the cabin and found Gilpin was dead, they'd probably have been on your trail anyway. Now you've had a hand in killin' some of 'em, they'll want to even the score. They'll want revenge.'

Bendix savoured the whiskey on his tongue. 'You might well be right,' he said, 'but it's still just a guess.'

'It's more than that,' Jennings replied. 'I recognized one of those coyotes in the saloon. He's wanted for murder and he's suspected of once ridin' with the Presidio Kid.'

Bendix's brow creased in concentration. 'If the Presidio Kid wants to even the scores with me, he'll want to do the same by you.'

'You're right. And since I don't aim to plunge this township into real trouble, I figure to hand things over to my deputy and leave town for a whiles. If I was to stay, the place could become a bloodbath.'

'I'd be around to help out,' Bendix said.

The marshal looked at him frankly, 'Sure appreciate that,' he said, 'but it seems a better idea for us both to leave town. Together.'

Bendix smiled. 'Be glad to have you along. But where are we headed?'

'It's a pity all three of those gunslicks got killed,' Jennings mused. 'If one of them had been alive, we might have got some information out of him.'

'We could head back to the cabin. If the Presidio Kid is following in Moss's wake and reckonin' to find Gilpin, that's where he'll go.'

The marshal was thinking. 'Makes sense,' he said. 'You say you spent time up there when Gilpin was still alive?'

'Yeah. Helped take care of him.'

'He never said anythin' to you . . . I mean about his time with the Presidio Kid?'

Bendix shook his head. 'Nothin' that I can recall. Maybe somethin' might occur to me if I look back on it real hard.'

'Seems to me those outlaws are takin' a lot of effort to come after Gilpin after all this time. I reckon there's more to it than just a settlin' of old scores.'

They both lapsed into silence, considering the situation. The marshal poured another glass of whiskey for each of them.

'I took a look at the horses those

owlhoots was riding,' he said. 'Two of them carried a Rocking-Horse brand. But I suspect they'd been interfered with. Likely the original brand was an Eleven Half-Circle. Maybe we should start by findin' where the Rocking-Horse spread is located and takin' us a look around. Expect we'll find the Eleven Half-Circle pretty close.'

Bendix tugged at his ear. 'Yeah,' he agreed. 'But where do we start? There could be a few places with either name.'

'Maybe so,' Jennings said. 'But the Presidio Kid didn't get his sobriquet for nothin'. I figure that the Rocking-Horse, assumin' it exists, is goin' to be not too far from Presidio.'

Bendix swallowed his whiskey and looked at the marshal. Suddenly they each broke into a laugh.

'Holy Moses,' Bendix said, 'I'm not too sure about your logic, but what the hell? I ain't been down to Texas in a long time. Be nice to resume acquaintances. Looks like we're bound for the Rio Grande.'

2

Marshal Ben Mercer sat in his office in the town of Horse Bend, north-west of Presidio. Things had been quiet for a considerable time but nevertheless the marshal was worried. Things seemed to be stirring out on the range. For the second time in as many days people had been coming to him with complaints about the Rocking-Horse spread: first Luke Grey from the Tumbling W and now Seb Coolidge from the Eleven Half-Circle. Their story was the same. Cattle had been disappearing from the range and they both blamed the Rocking-Horse, the biggest ranch in the territory. That in itself would have been significant, but the marshal had his own suspicions. He had had similar trouble from that direction before but it had blown over and things had settled down. There was still an uneasy atmosphere but nothing definite had occurred to disturb the relative tranquillity. Now the complaints were starting again. He wasn't even sure that it was his concern. Maybe it was a matter for the sheriff at the county seat. Maybe the Texas Rangers were the ones to handle it. But for the moment he felt it was down to him. Besides, he would feel foolish calling in outside assistance at this stage. Thinking about it, he resolved to pay a courtesy call on Miss Otilie at the Rocking-Horse. He hadn't been out there for a long while. It couldn't do any harm.

He had just come to this decision when he became aware of shouting outside, followed by a sudden outburst of noise. Getting to his feet, he strolled to the door, opened it and glanced down the street. A crowd had gathered outside the stagecoach office. The stage had just pulled in and the horses were stamping and snorting. A figure detached itself from the throng and came hurrying down the street towards him. It was

Harvey Scott, the stageline clerk.

'Marshal,' he gasped, 'there's been trouble. Some owlhoots attacked the stage. They've got away with the strongbox and the mail.'

'Anyone hurt?'

'They shot the guard. He's injured. I don't know how bad.'

'OK. I'm comin'.'

The two of them ran back down the street. When they arrived the injured guard had been carried inside the depot and laid on a bunk.

'Where are you hit?' Mercer snapped. 'Is it bad?'

'It's my leg,' the man gasped.

Mercer had begun to undo his bandanna to make a tourniquet when the doctor, a small thin man called Steiger, bustled into the room. A glance at the injured man told him what was required.

'Get the rest of them out of here,' he said to the marshal.

Curious people were crowding into the room, others were peering through a window. The marshal ushered the intruders out.

'Best get on with your business,' he advised. 'There's nothin' you can do around here.'

Most of the crowd began to melt away but a few of the more inquisitive lingered. Mercer found the driver seated on a bench in the waiting-room, taking a long pull from a flask.

'What happened?' Mercer asked.

The driver looked shaken-up but he was an old hand. He had experienced worse.

'About eight miles out of town,' he said. 'Just before the fork leading in the direction of the Rocking-Horse. Six riders hit us. We didn't have a chance.' He paused. 'Say, how's Clem? The shotgun guard.'

'Not sure,' Mercer replied, 'but I figure he'll pull through. The doc is with him now.' He stroked his chin. 'I don't suppose you recognized any of 'em?'

'Nope. It all happened so quickly. Besides, they had their neckerchiefs pulled up. One of 'em even wore some kind of a mask.'

'A mask?'

'Yeah, a sort of long black cloth with slits cut out for the eyes.'

Mercer looked thoughtful. 'Anythin' else about them?' he enquired.

'Nothin', only that they got away with the strongbox. I guess it was just lucky nobody got killed.'

'What about passengers?'

'What about them? Like I say, it was lucky nobody got killed.'

Mercer thought about asking some further questions but then decided against it. He could get information about the passengers from the clerk if he needed it and he might be able to pick up the trail of the owlhoots later. He put his hand for a moment on the driver's shoulder, then he re-entered the room where the wounded guard had been placed. The doctor had dug a bullet out of the fleshy part of his upper leg. The man had lost quite a lot of blood but the wound was clean and the doctor had bandaged it up and given him a dose of laudanum.

'He'll be OK,' the doctor confirmed in answer to Mercer's enquiring look. 'Might be a while before he's up on a horse again.'

Mercer went outside and took a look at the coach. The wood had been splintered and one of the windows was shattered but otherwise there was not a lot of damage. As he was examining it the clerk approached him.

'It's terrible,' he said. 'There was a lot of money in that strongbox. Nothin' like this has happened in a long time.'

The marshal was thinking: not since the bad days when the Presidio Kid and his gang had gone in for this type of thing.

'Let me have details,' he said.

He turned away, walked back to his office and mounted a bay gelding which was tied to the hitch-rack. He veered round, galloped past the stage depot and out into the country. It didn't take long to reach the point where the trail forked. There was plenty of evidence that something had occurred. The ground was rutted from the wheels of the coach and there was clear evidence of the owlhoots' horses. Traces of blood coloured the dust. Mercer could see where the riders had come down from some higher ground and where they had ridden afterwards. The trail led towards some rocky ground in the general direction of the Rocking-Horse. That didn't necessarily mean anything. The Rocking-Horse was a good way off. Keeping a close eye on the trail, Mercer followed the sign. At first it was easy but as he hit the rocky stretch it became harder to distinguish. A little further on he couldn't be sure which way the riders had gone. Someone more expert in tracking would probably have been able to do so, but he was no expert tracker. It seemed to him that the riders had probably split up. No doubt they had chosen this route on purpose to hide their trail. When he knew that he had lost it, the marshal halted the bay and rolled himself a cigarette.

From his vantage point he had a good view of the land rolling away in all directions. It was good grazing land and it seemed there was plenty for all. But then he thought about what the smaller ranchers had been telling him about the Rocking-Horse. As if that wasn't enough, he now had the stagecoach robbery to think about. It looked as though the peaceful times were changing. He took in a satisfying draught of tobacco and watched as a dark cloud spread its shadow over the prairie, as if hinting at trouble ahead. He thought about what the driver had told him. The Presidio Kid used to wear a mask.

★ ★ ★

The long ride from Wyoming to Texas suited Bendix. It felt a bit like old times, when he had ridden with Gilpin. From time to time his knee gave him trouble and he had to dismount to stretch his legs. Maybe it had been unwise to attempt so long a ride with his injured leg, but he wasn't complaining. For his part, Jennings was enjoying it too. He had been cooped up in Driftwood for too long. It was good to feel the wind in his face and to lie in the open with the stars for a ceiling. The heat of the day with its swarms of flies was made bearable by the knowledge of night's balm and the morning's coolness. But they needed to be alert. Only two days out of Driftwood they noticed a plume of dust in their wake.

'Could be somethin' or nothin',' Jennings commented.

Bendix nodded. 'Probably nothin'.'

When they camped that night Bendix woke up in the early hours, listening closely. The wind blew through the cottonwoods and willows and there was a plash of water from a nearby stream. Somewhere behind those sounds he thought he could discern the distant hoofbeats of horses. He was about to waken Jennings when he thought better of it. After what had happened at the cabin, maybe he was just being over-anxious. He checked his guns and lay down again, wakeful and looking up at the stars. When morning came and they had finished breakfast, he mentioned what he had heard to Jennings.

'Reckon you're right,' Jennings said. 'I thought I heard it too.'

Like Bendix had said, it was probably nothing. On the other hand, Jennings had recognized one of the gunmen in the shoot-out at the saloon as one of the Presidio Kid's sidekicks. They were half-expecting trouble.

It came the following day. The country had grown wilder, with patches of bunch grass interspersed with rocky outcrops and barren stretches of rock furrowed by sun, wind and rain. The trail that they were following had narrowed and they rode single file, Jennings taking the lead. Suddenly there was the *thwack* of a bullet and the echoing boom of a rifle. As his horse went down, Jennings rolled from the saddle and Bendix did likewise, pulling the steeldust down. As he did so more shots rang out.

'You OK?' Bendix called.

'I'm fine. Take cover.'

Bendix reached for his Winchester, drew it out of its scabbard and flung himself behind the shelter of some rocks. Jennings had already opened fire, but it wasn't clear where the shots had come from. Bendix called out to the steeldust and slapped it across its rear. The horse got to its feet and began to gallop away. Bendix was taking a risk and expected a fresh burst of fire to seek out the galloping horse, but there was none. Turning, he could see Jennings peering about for some sign of their attackers but the place was eerily still.

'See anythin'?' Bendix called.

'Nope!'

As if in answer to his question there suddenly came to their ears the sound of hoofs, moving away and fading into the distance.

'I don't get it,' Bendix called. 'They got us plumb pinned down.'

'Sure, but we got a good view of things from here. Maybe they didn't fancy takin' any chances.'

For what seemed a long while they lay still, careful in case any of the attackers remained behind. Eventually Bendix took off his hat and placed it on a nearby rock. It was an old trick but worth employing. Nothing happened. No rifle shot rang out and the hat remained unscathed. He reached out and took it back again.

'What do you reckon?' Bendix called.

'I reckon they've gone.'

Still they lay, not moving, as the afternoon wore by. Jennings's horse was not moving. High in the sky a buzzard began to circle.

'Can't stay here for ever,' Jennings called. 'Keep me covered.'

Quickly he got to his feet, leaped over the boulder behind which he had been crouched and ran towards Bendix. Bendix's Winchester was pressed against his shoulder and his finger was on the trigger but there was no need to squeeze it. Jennings halted and Bendix rose to his feet beside him.

'Looks like we were lucky this time,' he said.

Together they walked over to examine the horse. It had taken a shot clean in the chest and had probably died almost instantaneously.

Jennings turned to Bendix. 'Whoever took the horse out,' he said, 'was no mean shot. So why didn't they do a better job of killin' us?'

Bendix shrugged. 'Maybe they wanted to scare us.'

'Like I say, it don't make sense. It's almost like they wanted to keep us alive.' Bendix had a sudden illumination. 'Unless some of 'em think that I'm Gilpin.'

Jennings considered the idea. 'Hey, you could be right,' he said. 'Maybe they've been up to the cabin and figured Gilpin had gone.'

'There's the grave,' Bendix said.

'Yeah, but would they have even found it? You said it was among some trees back of the cabin.'

Bendix thought for a moment. 'And it was unmarked,' he said.

Jennings turned back to the dead horse. 'Well, we've got another problem to contend with right now. How's the steeldust gonna feel about takin' on two passengers?'

Bendix pursed his lips and whistled. After a few moments the steeldust came into view.

'What do you say, old fella?'

The horse whinnied.

'Glad you feel that way about it,' Bendix said. 'Wouldn't have made no difference anyway.'

⋆   ⋆   ⋆

It was mid-afternoon when Marshal Ben Mercer arrived at the boundary of the Rocking-Horse. In case anyone wasn't aware of the fact, there was a sign swaying in the breeze. It read:

Rocking-Horse
Sighted for Sharps .50
Shoots today, kills today.

A wry smile twisted the corners of the marshal's mouth. He recognized the play on the 'shoots today, kills tomorrow' slogan as applied to the Indians' use of the weapon. Although he had been on Rocking-Horse property at various times, he still felt a slight tingling of the spine as he rode on. Maybe the sign was for show; maybe someone had him in the sights of the buffalo gun right now. Perhaps he would have a word with Miss Otilie about it, although so far as he knew nobody had actually been the recipient of a bullet.

As he rode on he became aware again of just how big a spread it was. Soon he was passing cattle gathered in little groups, looking sleek and comfortable. Pretty soon they would be gathered in and heading up the Pecos valley on the first leg of the trail to Wyoming. Every now and again he slipped from the saddle to examine the brand but there was nothing to suggest that the brand markings might have been tampered with among the ones he looked at. Maybe Luke Grey and Seb Coolidge had been wrong.

Still, it didn't hurt to pay Miss Otilie a visit. He didn't see anyone apart from a couple of brush poppers in the distance, hazing some recalcitrant long-horns from the Brazos. That was unusual, he reflected. Most of the driving in bush country was done in the morning when it was cool. He guessed the round-up was well under way.

The Rocking-Horse ranch house was an impressive hacienda-style affair, with additional wings connected to the main building by covered walkways. Behind it were a number of outbuild-ings — stables, barns, corrals — and as he rode into the yard and stepped from the saddle, the door of the bunkhouse swung open and a lean youth stepped forward to take charge of the horse. A moment later the door of the ranch house opened and a tall man with a Mexican-style moustache appeared on the veranda.

'Ain't you got no business needs tendin' to in Horse Bend?' he remarked.

'My business for the moment is with Miss Otilie,' the marshal replied.

The man regarded Mercer closely before turning and going back through the door. After a few moments he reappeared.

'Miss Otilie is occupied at present,' he began, when suddenly a woman's figure appeared in the doorway behind him.

'It's all right, Craven,' she said. 'I've changed my mind.'

The man turned to her, then with a shrug made his way across the yard towards the bunkhouse.

'I won't say it's exactly nice to see you again, Marshal,' she said. 'But now you're here, won't you come on in?'

The marshal followed her inside the house. The main room was large and expensively furnished. In one corner was a bar and as she made towards it she asked the marshal what he would like to drink.

'Nothing for me, ma'am,' he said.

She indicated for him to take a seat and, ignoring his comment, brought him a glass of whiskey.

'Try it,' she said. 'I think you'll find it a little different from the usual forty-rod folks seem to enjoy around here.'

He took a sip. It was smooth and the glass was made of elegant cut-crystal.

'It's an imported Irish whiskey,' she said. 'I knew you would appreciate it.' She was drinking something golden in a long-stemmed glass and as she took a sip the marshal stole a glance at her. Despite knowing her, her appearance still fascinated him. At the same time, he felt awkward about looking at her too directly. It was hard to say exactly how old she was, but the marshal would have guessed she was in her early thirties. Although of average height, something about her gave her a powerful and impressive bearing and the elegant clothes she was wearing brought out the alluring grace of her figure. Her dark hair was short and sleek. At one time she must have been remarkably beautiful, Mercer thought, and for his part he felt that she still was. He didn't know whether other people would agree with him because down the length of her left cheek her face was badly scarred. There were various rumours about how it had happened. To Mercer it looked like a burn, but who could say for certain?

'Well,' she continued. 'I would imagine that you have a purpose in visiting the Rocking-Horse. Is there some way I can be of help?'

Not for the first time the marshal was beguiled by the tone of her voice. It was unusually deep and yet mellifluous and as if she had no interest other than in the person she was addressing. For a moment he didn't know how to reply.

'Let me guess,' she continued.

'You've had complaints from my neighbours. They're saying that some of my boys have been running off their cattle.' She paused and looked at Mercer through unflinching blue eyes.

'Am I right?' she said.

Mercer nodded. 'Miss Stevens,' he replied after some moments, 'I want you to know that I ain't takin' up any sort of a position in this matter. I've come out here just to clear the air and tell you straight what some folks has been thinkin'. Seems like you already know.'

She took another sip of her drink. 'I appreciate your neutrality,' she said. 'But you probably have an opinion. Go on, tell me what you think.'

'I think that it might be a good idea to put a stop right now to some of these rumours that have started circulating, before things take a step for the worse.'

'Step for the worse?'

'I think you know what I mean. I've seen things like this before. People start talkin', people get suspicious, one thing leads to another and before you know where you are you have a full-scale range war on your hands.'

'This isn't Lincoln County, Marshal. Besides, what reason would I have for stealing a few head of cattle? I'm the biggest rancher in the territory and beyond. I've got everything I need and more. Do you know how many acres and how many head of cattle I've got out there?'

The marshal shook his head. 'No ma'am, can't say that I do.'

'I got upwards of sixty thousand acres of prime grazing land. I got forty-five thousand cattle and a remuda of seven hundred and fifty saddle horses. I employ over two hundred cowboys and *vaqueros*. Without the Rocking-Horse this whole area would go to the dogs. So you tell me, what would I be doing rustling a few mangy longhorns from some two-bit fly-blown *rancheria*?'

She stopped. Mercer was surprised by the vehemence of her tone and when he caught another glance he noticed that the scar on her cheek was aflame. For a while there was silence while they both drank.

'I'm sorry,' she said. 'I didn't mean to sound angry. And I'm not denying that one of the boys might have acted without my knowledge and taken a cow for his supper. You know that sort of thing happens all the time. But as you can see, I've got nothing to gain from taking other folks' cows.'

The marshal rose to his feet. 'Thanks for giving me your attention,' he said.

'Any time,' she replied, accompanying him to the door. 'Glad to have helped clear things up.'

Any time? That's not the impression she gave out at first, the marshal reflected briefly. On the threshold he turned to her once more.

'Maybe you could do somethin' about that sign,' he remarked.

'Sign?'

'The one at the boundary to your property. It don't exactly give out a friendly signal.'

She paused as if in thought.

'Oh that!' she exclaimed. 'That was Craven's idea, I believe. You know my *segundo*?'

'I know him.'

'It was just his little joke. At the same time, it could have its uses in keeping out any unwanted visitors.'

The marshal glanced quickly into her eyes. There was no twinkle of humour in them.

'Just so long as it's only a warning,' he said. 'I'd hate to have to come out here to investigate a killing.'

She let out a hollow laugh. 'Of course not,' she said. 'Like I say, it was only his idea of a joke. It doesn't hurt to let the boys have their way now and again. If it bothers you so much, I'll have it taken down.'

The marshal stepped outside. At a nod from Miss Otilie one of the hands went to fetch his horse. When he had mounted he raised his hat to the woman standing on the veranda.

'Goodbye, Marshal,' she called. 'Come

back again soon.'

As he rode away he couldn't help thinking that it didn't seem likely she would let the hands have their way. Not over anything. Not ever.

Miss Otilie watched the marshal as he rode out of the yard. When he had gone she called to one of the hands to have her horse saddled. While that was being done she went indoors and changed into her riding-gear. When she came back out the horse was ready. It was a big buckskin, an unusual horse for a woman. She stepped into the saddle, rode slowly out of the yard, then turned in the opposite direction to the one she had seen the marshal follow.

Once clear of the ranch and out on the open range, she touched the horse lightly and set off at a steady jog. All her life she had been around horses and she was a very accomplished rider. Soon the jog had turned into a trot and then she was off at a full gallop. The horse seemed to respond without much urging and tore off, its hoofs thundering and spume flying from its nostrils. Apart from the odd longhorn or the occasional little group of cattle she had the wide range to herself.

At last she brought the buckskin to a halt, reached into her saddle-bags for a pair of binoculars and began to observe the terrain. For as far as she could see the land was hers. It gave her a sense of pride and satisfaction. She had started with nothing. Now she was the biggest rancher in the region.

For a long time she sat her horse and just looked at the scenery until eventually, along with the sense of satisfaction, she became conscious of another feeling, the old familiar feeling of restlessness. The marshal's words had brought on this sense of proprietorship and it was all well and good. But now she realized that for too long she had been missing the old life, the thrill of action, the elements of risk and uncertainty. Well, that was over now. No one could take the ranch away from her and she meant to enlarge it. At the same time it gave her cover for the other activities she had now resumed.

Not the least of them was this unexpected matter of Gilpin. She had thought that it had been over a long time ago. Now, out of the blue, it had come to life again. For a moment her heart seemed to skip a beat. She still felt something. Looking up, she could see the line cabin in the distance and, digging her spurs into the buckskin's flanks with an unnecessary emphasis, she rode on down to the shack.

She stepped down from the saddle, fastened the horse to a hitch rack, then opened the door with a key and entered.

The place might have looked like a shack from the outside but inside it was well and tastefully furnished with comfortable furniture, a bookcase with leather-bound volumes and a walnut escritoire. She flung herself down on a sofa, stretched her legs and laid her head back against a cushion. She liked to use this place as a retreat, a place where she could be alone and not have to concern herself with any of the affairs of the Rocking-Horse. She had quiet in order to plan things and work out what her next move might be. And right now, she needed time to think.

She got to her feet and moved to a little adjoining room that served as a bedchamber. Pausing in front of a mirror, she forced herself to look at her reflection. For a moment or two she stood immobile, till suddenly she turned away with a cry, clutching at the scar on her cheek. Tears were in her eyes. Sometimes she was made to remember that whatever else she might be, she was still a woman.

★　★　★

It was late in the afternoon when the steeldust carrying Bendix and Jennings came in sight of a small group of ramshackle buildings with a corral of peeled poles back of them. In the corral were a couple of tired-looking horses but there was no other sign of life. The steeldust's ears were pricked and he seemed nervous. Bendix brought the horse to a halt.

'I don't like it,' he said.

'Me neither,' Jennings replied.

They both dismounted and Bendix hobbled the steeldust. Then they crept forward, keeping low and taking advantage of whatever cover they could. When they reached a point where they could go no further without being seen, Bendix turned to Jennings.

'There should be some activity,' he said.

'Looks like there's been some,' Jennings replied. 'The yard is pretty well scuffed up. I'd say a number of riders were here recently.'

They looked at one another.

'The Presidio Kid?' Bendix suggested.

'Either him or some of his owlhoot gang. Looks to me like the same bunch of bushwhackers as jumped us came by this way.'

'And left their callin' card,' Bendix muttered.

For a few minutes they continued to observe the place.

'I don't reckon there's anybody there,' Bendix said. 'At least, not alive.' He drew the Smith & Wesson from its holster. 'Give me cover,' he said. 'I'm goin' to make a run for the door.'

Jennings shook his head. 'Ain't you forgettin' something?'

Bendix gave him a puzzled look.

'You ain't runnin' nowhere with that leg of yours. You do the coverin' and let me do the other bit.'

Taking a deep breath, Jennings burst out into the open and began running hard. Despite what Bendix had said he was half-anticipating a burst of lead to greet him and he swerved as he ran. There was no firing, however, and as he approached the door he barely broke stride but crashed into it with his shoulder. There was no resistance; it sprang open and as it did so Jennings threw himself into a somersault, landing on his knee. His gun swept the room. It took only a moment for him to realize that there was no danger. Lying on the floor were the bodies of a middle-aged man and woman. They had been shot a number of times. At the back of the room was a narrow doorway; when he peered inside he found another body, that of an elderly man. Lying beside him was a gun. It had been fired twice and there was a bullet hole in the ceiling. At least the old man had been able to offer some resistance, Jennings thought. He guessed that the bullet might have found its mark because there were spots of blood leading back into the main room; it was unlikely that they came from any of the dead. Hearing footsteps behind him, Jennings spun round, but it was only Bendix.

'Reckon we were right about those owlhoots,' Jennings said. 'They may have given us a chance, but they sure didn't do the same for these folks.'

Looking around, it seemed to them that nothing had been touched or interfered with. It looked like a case of sheer murder.

'They left the horses,' Bendix said.

'I guess they considered them just too broke-down to worry about. Lucky for us.'

Night had fallen by the time Bendix and Jennings had buried the three corpses, but neither of them felt like staying around the place. They gathered together a few things that might come in useful and loaded them on to one of the horses. Then Jennings saddled up the other and they rode out into the darkness.

3

Miss Otilie Stevens was sitting on the veranda when Craven, her foreman, rode into the yard.

'Lawson's back,' he said.

Miss Otilie nodded.

'Him and the rest of the boys will be here directly,' Craven added.

'That's fine. Carry on with whatever you're doin'.'

Craven stepped into leather, turned and rode off. Miss Otilie began to rise from her seat but then sat back again. She mustn't give anything away. She mustn't let anyone suspect the thrill of anticipation which had shot through her at Craven's words. Settling herself down, she waited for Lawson's arrival. Presently a group of riders appeared in the distance, raising a cloud of dust as they approached the ranch house and rode into the yard. The foremost rider dismounted and stood in front of Miss Otilie with the horse's reins held in his hands.

'Ma'am,' he said, touching his hand to the rim of his hat.

'See to the horses,' Miss Otilie said to Lawson, 'then tell the boys to get somethin' to eat at the bunkhouse. Report back to me in twenty minutes.'

'One of the boys got shot,' Lawson said.

Miss Otilie glanced up. Swaying in the saddle, one of the riders was clutching at his shoulder.

'I'll get Jones to take a look,' she said. 'He's as good as any doctor, with a horse or a man.' She looked again at the bunched riders. 'Seems to me you left somebody behind somewhere,' she said.

Lawson shuffled and looked awkward. 'There was an incident,' he said. 'Some of the boys got into trouble.'

She looked up anxiously. 'Trouble?'

'It weren't nothin' to do with Gilpin,' Lawson replied. 'From what I can gather, Dicks and a couple of the boys had a run-in with the marshal. In a place called Driftwood.'

Miss Otilie's anger was offset by the sense of relief she felt that the incident, as Lawson described it, had not involved Gilpin.

'Dicks was always a hot-head,' she replied. 'He had it comin' to him.'

When the riders had dispersed Miss Otilie went inside the ranch house and poured herself a drink. She set one out for Lawson. Presently there was a knock on the door.

'Come in!' she called.

Lawson entered, still looking a little sheepish. He had slicked himself up a little and looked a lot more presentable than when he had first rode in off the trail. Miss Otilie waved him to a seat next to where his drink stood on a low table. For a few minutes there was silence. Lawson wasn't sure of his ground and Miss Otilie didn't want to be the first to speak. They both sipped their drinks.

'Guess you want to know what

happened?' Lawson began at last.

She looked at him with her piercing eyes.

'Well,' he stuttered, 'we found the cabin without too much bother. All we had to do was keep tailin' Moss. Trouble was, that's all we found.'

'What about Gilpin? Was he not there?'

'There was nothin', ma'am, although it seemed the place had been occupied till fairly recently. There was food on the shelves and ashes in the grate. We stuck around for a whiles in case somebody turned up.'

'I trust you kept out of sight?'

'Yes of course, ma'am.'

'And what about Moss?'

'I don't know what happened to Moss. He just kinda disappeared.'

'Surely it would have been easy to keep track of him?' Miss Otilie snapped. Lawson was looking and feeling very uncomfortable. 'So you're telling me you found no trace of Gilpin? Did you search the place?'

'Yeah, but there was nothin' to

indicate that he was ever even there.'

Miss Otilie's throat was dry. She sipped at her drink.

'It's my opinion, ma'am, that we just missed Gilpin.'

She swung her gaze back to him.

'There were fresh horse tracks leading down from the mountain. Taken with the fact that we lost touch with Moss, I reckon Gilpin either killed him or at least got wind that he was in the vicinity and rode off just before we got there. One way or the other, I guess Moss must have spooked him.'

'Maybe it was you and your incompetence that spooked him,' she replied.

Lawson didn't answer and, as Miss Otilie was thinking over what he had just told her, silence once again descended. Miss Otilie had seemed to forget that he was there till she suddenly sat up once more.

'All right, Lawson,' she said. 'You can go now. But I might want to speak to you again later. Make sure you don't go too far.'

Lawson arose with alacrity, anxious to escape from the room. 'Thank you, ma'am,' he mumbled and made quickly for the door.

When he was gone Miss Otilie remained seated for a long time, deep in thought. If there was any truth in the idea that Gilpin was to be found in that cabin in the mountains, and he had been spooked into leaving, where was he now? If he knew that they were on his trail what would he do? Maybe he would simply seek for new cover. But maybe he would come to the conclusion that it was no longer any use to run, to hide. He might reason that the time had come to take the bull by the horns and settle accounts, in which case he could be headed for Texas right now.

A frisson of anticipation shot through her. Things were moving fast. It was getting to be more and more like the old days and she realized afresh how much she had missed them during her long incarceration at the Rocking-Horse. The stage hold-up had just been the start. The Presidio Kid was ready to ride again.

★   ★   ★

It was early in the morning when Bendix and Jennings rode into the township of Horse Bend. After arranging for their horses to be looked after at the livery stables they made for the nearest restaurant for breakfast. While they were eating, Bendix glanced out of the window. Across the street a buckboard was drawn up outside the general store. Nearby a couple of cowboys were loafing.

'Wonder what they're doin' in town so early?' Bendix commented.

'Who?' Jennings said.

'Two cowpokes. Can't say as I like the looks of 'em.'

Just then the waitress came by with a pot of coffee. She poured them each a cup and then, bending, looked out of the window.

'They're from the Rocking-Horse,'

she said. Bendix glanced up. 'Sorry. I couldn't help overhearing what you said.'

Bendix smiled. 'Sure is good coffee,' he said.

'The Rocking-Horse?' Jennings repeated.

'You must be new in town,' the waitress replied. 'The Rocking-Horse is by far the biggest spread around here. Didn't used to be. All the more remarkable when you consider it's run by a woman.'

Bendix's hand paused on its way to conveying the cup of coffee to his mouth.

'A woman?' he said. 'I guess that is a little unusual. What's her name?'

'She's called Miss Otilie, Miss Otilie Stevens. She tends to keep herself to herself. Don't get into town too often.'

'So how do you know those two are in her employ?'

'That's easy. Miss Otilie may be a stranger to town, but those two are frequent visitors.' She bent down to get a better view through the window. 'The one on the right is Jud Wilkins. The other one, in the red shirt, is Vin Barrett.'

Bendix pondered her words for a moment but before he could ask the waitress any further questions another customer came through the door and she moved away. He looked out of the window once again. The door to the general store opened and a young woman appeared, carrying a bag of groceries. Behind her was a small man wearing an apron and carrying another bag. Together they lifted the bags into the buckboard. The lady turned to thank him and he made his way back into the shop. She looked up and down the street. She was quite small and thin and she wore a plain calico dress and a bonnet from which hung two ribbons. The effect was plain enough but there was something about her which held Bendix's attention. As he watched she glanced towards the restaurant as though she was considering coming over. She must have thought better of it because she turned and began to walk around the wagon.

At the same moment the two cowboys moved up beside her. She paused, then made to continue, but one of them, the man in the red shirt the waitress had referred to as Vin Barrett, stood in her way. The lady looked up into his face. The other cowboy had moved up behind her and as Bendix watched he turned and spat into the dust. Barrett seemed to be saying something. Bendix didn't wait any further. In a flash he was on his feet and out of the door of the café. As he approached all three of the actors in the little drama looked up.

'You're crowdin' the lady,' Bendix said.

The two cowboys looked at each other and then laughed. 'Is that so?' Barrett turned to the woman. 'Is that true?' he said. 'Are we crowdin' you, ma'am?'

The woman looked from one to the other and then to Bendix. 'It's all right,' she said. 'I can handle things.'

With those words she stepped past Wilkins and began to climb on to the buckboard. When she was in the seat she turned to Bendix.

'I appreciate your concern,' she said.

Barrett looked up at her. 'Don't forget what we were talkin' about,' he said. 'Make sure your father gets the message.'

'You are a contemptible reptile,' she replied, 'and I have no intention of doing any such thing.'

The look that accompanied her words was withering and it had its effect in goading her assailants. With a scowl on his face, Barrett made a move as if to haul her down from the buckboard, but in the same instant Bendix's fist shot out and caught him square on the jaw, sending him hurtling into the road. He was on his feet in seconds, throwing himself towards Bendix. Bendix was too quick for him and stepped aside but his weak knee gave way beneath him and he fell to the ground. Before he could regain his feet Barrett's hand had reached for his gun but Bendix was quicker. Almost simultaneously the two shots rang out but it was Barrett who was hit. Staggering back from the impact, he was about to fire again when Bendix's second shot caught him in the chest. He slumped to the floor, his eyes glazing over and blood pumping into the dust. Bendix was on his feet and swivelling towards Wilkins. Everything had happened so quickly that Wilkins had been taken by surprise, but his gun was in his hand, about to spit lead, when a shout rang out across the street.

'I wouldn't do that if I were you!'

Wilkins looked up to see a man standing in the doorway of the restaurant with a six-gun in his hand.

'Drop it now or you're a dead man.'

Bendix had been disorientated but now he had his bearings.

'Do as the man says!' he snapped. 'I got you in my sights now as well.'

Wilkins hesitated for only a moment

longer before he let the gun fall from his hand. Bendix turned to the lady sitting high on the buckboard.

'Apologies, ma'am,' he said.

Apart from a slight involuntary tremor, she seemed to be in control of herself.

'None of it was your fault,' she said. She looked at him again; her eyes were limpid and brown. 'I think you've been wounded.'

Bendix felt blood running down his cheek. Feeling his head, he realized that his brow had been creased by Barrett's bullet. Another fraction of an inch and his head would have been blown off.

'It's nothin',' he said, then fell to the ground. As he lay in the dust the last thing of which he was conscious was a pair of brown eyes looking anxiously into his own.

When he came round he was lying on a bed in a strange place. There were faces around him, among whom he recognized the familiar features of Jennings.

'Where am I?' he asked.

'Take it easy,' Jennings replied. 'You took a knock to the head, but you'll be OK. Ain't that right, Doc?'

The man so addressed got to his feet. 'Sure, he'll be fine. But when will you boys ever learn? You were plumb lucky this time, but who knows about the next?'

Bendix smiled his appreciation and the doctor left the room along with somebody else. Only Jennings remained.

'Funny,' Bendix said. 'I seem to have heard that before. About bein' lucky.'

'You said it yourself. Let's hope we both stay that way.'

'What happened? Where are we?'

'We're guests of Mr Seb Coolidge and his daughter Miranda on his ranch, the Eleven Half-Circle. Seems like you got hurt offerin' her some kind of service.' There was a grin on Jennings's face.

'Guess we save on hotel bills,' he said. 'You sure spoilt breakfast, though.' Bendix raised himself on one elbow but his head throbbed and he lay back again. Just then the door opened and the lady with the brown eyes appeared.

'Is he all right?' she said, addressing Jennings.

'I'm all right,' Bendix replied. 'Just a bit of a headache.'

She turned to him. 'I'm sorry,' she said. 'I didn't realize you were awake.'

Bendix sat up again, this time slowly, and lay with his head propped on a pillow.

'Sure didn't intend puttin' you to all this bother,' he said.

'It's no bother. You and your friend are welcome.'

'We'll be out of your way soon. In the meantime, let us officially introduce ourselves. I'm Clugh Bendix and this is Will Jennings.'

The woman smiled. 'Yes, I know,' she said. 'And I'm Miranda Coolidge. My father owns this ranch, the Eleven Half-Circle.'

Bendix and Jennings exchanged glances. They were both thinking of the Rocking Chair and those horse brands that seemed to have been tampered with. Miranda moved towards the door, hesitated with her fingers on the handle.

'I appreciate what you did, Mr Bendix,' she said. 'And you too, Mr Jennings. There's not many in town would have stood up to those two coyotes.'

Bendix looked up at her. 'I gather they were from the Rocking-Horse,' he said.

'Yes, you're right. What do you know about the Rocking-Horse?'

'Only what I've been told. That it's the biggest spread in the region and run by a woman. Seems like she's got some mean *hombres* ridin' for her.'

'She don't frighten us,' Miranda said.

'Is that what those two were tryin' to do? Frighten you?'

Miranda thought for a moment as though she was pondering her reply, then she shook her head.

'Don't go concernin' yourself about the Rocking-Horse,' she answered. 'That's our business. You just make sure you clear your head.' She went out, shutting the door behind her.

'I wonder what she meant by that?' Bendix said. 'I'd like to know what that skunk said to her.'

'Whatever he said and whatever's goin' on,' Jennings replied, 'it looks like we've fetched up at the right place. Now all we need is an appearance from the Presidio Kid.'

'Yeah,' Bendix answered. 'And I reckon we will see him before long.'

* * *

Back in Horse Bend, Marshal Mercer was sitting in his office, thinking things over. To add to his troubles, he now had one of Miss Otilie's riders dead and a second kicking his heels in the jail-house. It seemed to be one thing after another. Were they connected? And who were these two newcomers whom Miranda had taken off to the Eleven Half-Circle? There was only one way to find out. He saddled up his horse and set out for the ranch. When he got there he found Seb Coolidge already standing on the veranda.

'I've been expectin' you, Marshal,' he said. 'Come right on in.'

Mercer followed him into the house and without any preamble Coolidge began to question him.

'Well, Marshal, what further proof do you need now?' he said when he had finished. Mercer looked at him enquiringly. 'What about that no-good coyote you got in the jailhouse? Leastways I imagine that's where he is. Has he said anythin'? Let me come down there. I'll soon make him talk.'

'I'm not sure what you're on about,' Mercer replied. 'I've come out here to have a word with the two *hombres* I understand you've taken under your wing.'

Coolidge looked at him. 'I guess you must know what happened? If it hadn't have been for Mr Bendix in particular I don't know what the consequences might have been for Miranda. Bringing them back here was the least I could do.'

'I guess we're comin' at the same thing but from a different angle,' the marshal said. 'You better tell me just what exactly occurred when Miss Miranda came out of the general store.'

'What exactly occurred? Sure, I'll tell you just what occurred. My daughter was set upon by two stinkin' polecats belongin' to the Rocking-Horse. They threatened her and they threatened me and I want to know just what you intend doin' about it.'

'Once I know the facts — ' the marshal began, then he was interrupted by Miranda entering the room. Her father turned and walked quickly up to her.

'Miranda,' he said, 'go back. There's no need for you to be upset all over again.' He faced the marshal. 'Well, I guess you can feel pleased with yourself that you've caused my daughter to have to go over this once more.'

'It's all right,' Miranda said. 'I'm not

upset. I appreciate your concern, but really, I'm OK.' She turned to the marshal. 'What is it you want to know?'

The marshal looked apologetic. 'I'm sorry, Miss Miranda. I just want to know the facts in the case.'

'Well, let me tell you then. I was in Horse Bend collecting some supplies. When I came out of the general store to put my purchases in the buckboard, I was confronted by two Rocking-Horse hands. They accosted me and wouldn't allow me to take my seat on the buck-board. One of them, I believe his name is Barrett, said he had a message for my father.' She paused.

'Yes, Miss Miranda, and what was that?'

She looked at her father before replying. 'They said that if he didn't accept the offer Miss Otilie Stevens had made for the Eleven Half-Circle, they would burn us out.'

Again she hesitated.

'He also said something personal to me which I would rather not repeat.'

Coolidge stepped forward. 'That's

enough,' he shouted. 'Marshal, can't you see that you're upsetting my daughter?'

She turned to him and placed her hand on his arm. 'Really,' she said, 'it's all right. It would take a lot more than that to upset me.'

She smiled at her father. 'What I couldn't understand,' she said, 'was what he said about Miss Otilie having made you an offer for the Eleven Half-Circle. It's not true, Father, is it?'

Seb Coolidge ran his hand through his hair, then sat down on a sofa.

'I'm sorry,' he replied. 'I should have said something. I should have told you but I didn't want you to worry. Besides, I'd already decided to ignore it.'

'Ignore what?' the marshal said. 'What is this about an offer for the Eleven Half-Circle?'

'What difference does it make?' Coolidge said. 'I have no intention either of accepting it or of being driven off my own land.'

'When did she make this offer?' Mercer said.

'Just recently. It's not worth discussing. The price she offered is only a fraction of what the place is worth. Besides which, I built this spread from nothin'. It may not amount to much in comparison with the Rocking-Horse, but it's my land and I have no intention of ever leavin'.'

'Of course not,' Miranda put in. 'And I have lived here all my life and I intend staying here too.' She turned to her father. 'I'm so glad you said that. The two of us together will be more than a match for the Rocking-Horse.'

Coolidge turned to the marshal. 'One other thing I guess you should know. Luke Grey from the Tumbling W has received a similar offer. He has apparently taken a different attitude from mine and is considering acceptin' it. One way and another, looks like the Rocking-Horse is set to expand even further and take over the Tumbling W.'

The marshal's face expressed concern. Although he had been trying to take a middle course and avoid bias in any disputes between the local ranchers, he couldn't help feel that the Rocking-Horse was pushing things too hard. Just then they were interrupted by the appearance of Bendix.

'Shouldn't you be in bed?' Miranda queried.

'I'm fine now,' Bendix said. His words were not convincing as he wobbled slightly in the doorway. 'I know it ain't none of our business,' Bendix continued, 'but the door was open and we couldn't help overhearing what you were saying. I just want you to know that if it comes to any sort of fightin', you got me and Jennings right behind you.'

'Nobody said anythin' about fightin',' the marshal said.

Coolidge looked at Bendix. 'Thanks,' he said. 'Sure appreciate your offer. Let's hope it don't come to that but it's good to know you got friends.'

The marshal rose to his feet. 'Now let's just stay calm,' he said.

'In view of what happened to my

daughter, I'd say we'd gone beyond that,' Coolidge commented.

'Let me take a ride over to the Rocking-Horse,' the marshal said. 'See just what this is all about. I'm sure there must have been some sort of misunderstanding. Maybe I'll call in at the Tumbling W as well, have a word with Luke.'

'If so, you'd better make it soon,' Coolidge said. 'I don't know whether he's signed any papers, but if it's all done legal now there ain't nothin' anyone can do about it.'

'I've known Luke a long time. He ain't the one to rush into anythin'.' The marshal turned to Bendix and Jennings. 'You seem to have stirred somethin' up,' he said. 'If you don't mind me askin', I'd like to know just what your plans are right now.'

Bendix and Jennings exchanged glances. 'Ain't rightly too sure — ' Jennings began.

Suddenly Coolidge interrupted. 'They're workin' for me,' he said.

The marshal looked at him. 'Since when?' he rapped.

'Since right now. Ain't that correct, boys?'

Bendix and Jennings were taken by surprise but catching a wink from Coolidge they were quick to agree.

'Yeah,' Bendix replied. 'Sure is. Just tell us what you want doin'.'

The marshal looked suspiciously at them both. 'You boys got any experience of ranchin'?' he enquired.

'Plenty.'

The marshal moved towards the door. 'I'd better get goin',' he said. Turning to Bendix and Jennings he added, 'I'll be wantin' to have a chat with you boys. Call in to my office next time you're in town.'

'Fine by us,' Bendix said and Jennings nodded. Bendix was reminded of his first encounter with Jennings. He had been suspicious of Bendix then. Maybe that was just the way with lawmen; maybe it had to be that way if they were to survive.

The marshal mounted his horse and rode away. When he had gone Coolidge turned to Bendix.

'Hope you didn't mind my little intervention,' he said. 'I figured it would square things with Mercer, at least for a time.'

'We sure don't mean to impose,' Bendix replied.

Coolidge gave him an astute look. 'I figure you boys got some reason for bein' in Horse Bend. You could be needin' some place to stay.'

'We'll book in at the hotel,' Bendix said.

'No you won't. Besides, how would that look to the marshal? Get your things and put them in the bunkhouse.'

Bendix hesitated. He turned to Jennings.

'Seems like a real good offer,' Jennings said.

Miranda had left the room after the marshal's departure. Now she reappeared in the doorway.

'We'd like you to stay,' she said.

'You'd be doin' us a favour. At least stay till you're better.'

Bendix was looking a little white. His head was burning and his knee hurt.

'Go and lie down. I'll bring you some beef broth. Later on I'll take you across to the bunkhouse.'

Bendix smiled. 'OK,' he said. 'We'll take up your offer, but with one proviso.'

'Yeah, what's that?' Coolidge said.

'That you'll let us help around here and if matters really come to a head, that we can stick around and offer whatever support we can.'

'Then it's a deal,' Coolidge confirmed.

Later, as he sat alone, Coolidge thought over Bendix's words about things coming to a head. That was the way Coolidge felt. Whatever hopes the marshal might have of avoiding trouble, Coolidge couldn't help feeling that it was too late, that somehow a step had been taken which meant there was no going back. Bendix seemed to have an instinctive feel for the situation. If they were right, it would be more than useful to have Bendix and Jennings around. They had acquitted themselves well in the confrontation with Barrett and Wilkins. Those two were mean *hombres*, same as a lot of other Rocking-Horse riders. And from the way that they had handled their guns, it looked like Bendix and Jennings could use them. More important, he liked the cut of their jib.

It was next morning that Bendix brought up the subject of cattle rustling. He and Jennings had breakfasted at the bunkhouse and, coming on top of a good night's rest, Bendix was feeling a lot better. Walking outside, they saw Coolidge standing by one of the corrals which contained a good number of cattle. They wandered over to join him.

'We're a bit behind already,' Coolidge said. 'From what I can gather, the Rocking-Horse is about to start up the trail any time now.'

'What about the other ranch?'

'The Tumbling W? Not sure. Guess they'll be goin' with the Rocking-Horse unless Luke has changed his mind.'

'The Rocking-Horse seems to have a wide influence,' Bendix said. 'In fact, it's because we found the brand on some horses back in Driftwood that we came on down here.'

'Is that right?'

Briefly Bendix told Coolidge what had happened to bring him and Jennings to Wyoming.

'Seemed to me,' Jennings said, 'that those brands had been interfered with. I understand you've been losin' some cattle. It would fit. It didn't take us long to work out the Rocking-Horse was probably originally the Eleven Half-Circle.'

'That was very astute of you,' Coolidge replied. 'Matter of fact, I'm pretty sure the Rocking-Horse has been takin' my cattle.'

'Have you told the marshal?'

'Sure. He said he was goin' to visit

Miss Otilie at the Rocking-Horse. Nothin' will come of it. It's happened before. I think he just wants to avoid trouble on the range. Can't say as I blame him.'

'This Miss Otilie,' Bendix said. 'She sounds an interesting lady. What can you tell us about her?'

'Well, not much really. She took over the spread not too long ago; not more than two, three years. It was a lot smaller then. She's built it up to what it is now.'

'Must have taken a lot of cash, one way and another,' Jennings commented. 'She must have had money.'

'Yeah, I've sometimes wondered about that. She's got her hand in one or two other pies as well. I figure she's a wealthy woman or else she's got backing. There's been some rumours but I don't give 'em no credence.'

'What sort of rumours?'

'Well, there were stories that she originally made her pile runnin' cows over the border into Mexico.'

'Do you have any dealings with her?'

'Nope. Keeps herself pretty much to herself. Some folks say it's because of her scar. Don't get me wrong, she's still not a bad-lookin' woman. But somewhere along the line her face got badly scarred up. Rumour is that she feels bad about it. Doesn't like people to see it.'

'Goin' back to that rustlin' business,' Bendix said. 'Since the marshal ain't done much, have you done anythin' yourself?'

'I like to keep the right side of the law,' Coolidge replied. 'Besides, the Rocking-Horse is too big. They hold all the aces.'

'We'll see about that.'

Coolidge turned to him. 'What you got in mind, Bendix?'

'Well, seems to me we need proof in the first place that it's been goin' on. Why don't we stake out one of the likeliest places it might be happenin' and see for ourselves whether we're right. Where would you suggest, Coolidge?

You must have some idea.'

Coolidge looked at Bendix with a smile on his lips and a glint in his eye.

'You know, you're right,' he said. 'I bin sittin' on my hands for too long. It's about time we started doin' somethin'.'

He looked up and called over to a cowboy who was making his way to the bunkhouse.

'Clancy, if you see Jensen, ask him to step over here.'

After a few minutes the foreman arrived and Coolidge had a few words with him. Glancing at Bendix, the foreman replied with a grin on his lips to match Coolidge's.

'I reckon the top range would be a good place to start,' he said. 'It ain't the best grazin' but the ground is broken. There's plenty of cover and it abuts right on to Rocking-Horse territory.'

'OK,' Coolidge said. 'We'll give it a try.'

'Why don't we four head out that way tonight?' Bendix said. 'Could be real int'restin'.'

As they went their separate ways, Bendix was thinking about Miss Otilie Stevens. Some intriguing points had been raised about her and the Rocking-Horse. He wondered whether there was anything in the rumours about her having been involved in running cattle over the Rio Grande into Mexico. Wasn't that where the Presidio Kid used to operate, and hadn't that been one of his various activities?

4

The first thing that Marshal Mercer did when he arrived back in Horse Bend was to pay a visit to the offices of Drake Jordan, attorney-at-law. Although it was late in the afternoon the lawyer was still hard at work. When the marshal was announced he sighed deeply, took some papers from his desk and stashed them in a chest of drawers in one corner of the room. He felt a degree of irritation. From time to time their paths had crossed and it was not usually to his advantage. In fact there was an unspoken antipathy between Jordan and Mercer, although neither of them would have wanted to show it.

'Come on in, Marshal,' he said as Mercer came through the doorway. 'As you can see, I'm hard at it but I've always got time to see you.'

'Appreciate it,' the marshal replied. 'I

don't intend takin' up much of your time.'

'A drink?' Jordan said.

The marshal waved his hand. 'Let me get straight to the point,' he said. 'Fact of the matter is, I just heard today that Grey is fixin' to sell up.'

Jordan did not reply.

'I understand that the Rocking-Horse stands to gain a lot by the transaction — that Miss Otilie is indeed the proposed purchaser.'

Jordan was still silent but, observing him closely, Mercer thought he detected a bead of sweat on the attorney's brow.

'I wonder if you could confirm the story.'

The lawyer fidgeted with his hands. 'What makes you think I would know anything about this?'

'Because you're the only lawyer in town. 'Most any business comes through you.'

'That may be so, but there is still such a thing as professional privacy.'

'Come off it,' Mercer said. 'There's

no big secret involved in any of this. Besides, I represent the law as well as you.'

'That may be so, but I fail to see what interest you would have in the matter.'

'Everything that happens around here is my interest,' Mercer replied.

'Why don't you ask Grey?'

'I fully intend to. But you haven't answered my question.'

The lawyer's brows drew together in a frown. He seemed to consider the matter closely.

'All right,' he said. 'I guess you're right. It will be common knowledge soon enough. Yes, Mr Grey is selling the Tumbling W and Miss Otilie Stevens is the purchaser.'

Mercer sat up. 'I want you to delay finalizing the paperwork,' he said, 'until I've had a word with Grey.'

'I'm afraid that is out of the question. This is purely a commercial matter. I intend dealing with it in the customary fashion.'

'Do as I say,' Mercer snapped. 'Grey

is an old friend of mine and I want to check this matter out with him.'

'What is there to check?'

'How much is he selling for?'

'That is confidential. I can't possibly divulge such information.'

'That's fine,' Mercer said, getting to his feet. 'You must have lots of business in hand. You just said yourself that you've been hard at it. Just make sure you don't rush this through.'

The lawyer looked uncomfortable. 'I don't think there's a lot of point in visiting the Tumbling W. I wouldn't advise it. You'll be just wasting your time and I'm sure you have more pressing matters to deal with. The transaction is well in hand.'

'Just don't do anything till you hear from me.'

Jordan seemed about to argue the matter further but then he shrugged.

'And how long will that be?'

'Not long,' Mercer replied.

Going out of the room and down the stairs, he could scarcely repress a shudder. There was something reptilian about Jordan. And it was for sure that he would be a beneficiary of any deal that was under way.

Bendix, Jennings, Coolidge and Clancy rode into the broken country of the upper range. It was a dark night with no moon and only a few stars coming and going between scudding clouds. There was a spring hidden among cotton-woods and willows, which Coolidge figured would make a good hiding-place. From there they could survey the rough country where mesquite thickets concealed old mossyhorns down in the draws. They sat their horses, talking quietly now and then, but generally maintaining silence. Bendix drew out his pouch of tobacco and was about to build himself a smoke when he thought better of it. He didn't want to take any chance of giving their position away. Time passed. Apart from the occasional snicker of one of the horses, there was no sound other than the soughing of the wind in the trees and a faint trickle of water. The cloud cover increased until it was difficult to discern anything at all out on the range.

'Seems like we might have got this wrong,' Jennings whispered, when suddenly Coolidge held up his hand, his finger pointing away into the blackness.

'Over there,' he said.

They all strained their eyes but could see nothing.

'What was it?'

'I don't know. A kind of faint glow. Maybe I'm imaginin' things.'

Bendix looked hard. Beyond the trees the blackness of night was smudged with dim shapes and shadows. It was easy to imagine things moving out there, easy to let stretched nerves reveal presences that had no existence.

'There!' Coolidge snapped.

Bendix followed the line of his outstretched finger and this time he thought that he, too, could make out a very faint glow.

'A campfire,' Bendix said. 'I reckon it's a campfire.'

The four of them exchanged glances in the dark. They were thinking the same thing. What would a campfire be doing out here in the rough country?

'Let's get a little closer, see if we can take a look.'

Touching their spurs to their horses' flanks, they emerged from the shelter of the cottonwoods and began to ride slowly in the general direction from which they thought they had seen the campfire's glow. Moving slowly, they continued riding but they could still see nothing. A stretch of rising ground interposed itself and coming round it, they stopped to take another look about but without success. Bendix rode his horse up the slope, hoping to get a vantage point from which he might survey their surroundings, but there was nothing before him but a sea of black. Either they had been mistaken all along, or if there was a campfire, it had been doused. They carried on riding for a time till Coolidge signalled for them to halt.

'We ain't doin' a lot of good like this,'

he said. 'We'll make camp for the rest of the night and see what we can find when mornin' comes.'

They had come prepared and, having found a suitable hollow, they settled down for the rest of the night, resisting the temptation to light a fire themselves. When dawn came they soon had a fire going and a pot of coffee on the coals. They ate some jerky and biscuit, knowing that they weren't too far from the ranch house and a decent meal later.

The sky was filled with clouds and rain was in the air when they climbed into the saddle and rode out. They moved slowly, scouting for traces of the campfire they thought they had seen during the night. After what seemed a long time they eventually came upon it. It hadn't been easy to find. Whoever had been there had taken care to remove its traces and if they hadn't have been searching for it they would probably have passed it by. Bendix reckoned there had been four men but it was difficult to read their sign.

'Four men,' Coolidge said. 'A neat number for some illicit range brandin'. A roper, a couple of flankers and a brander.'

'You're probably right,' Bendix said. 'If so, they must be pretty confident, not even waitin' till they'd run 'em off.'

'And not settlin' for just an earmark either,' Clancy added.

'Well, we may not have caught anybody actually at the rustlin',' Coolidge said, 'but we got enough circumstantial evidence to persuade me. Let's get on back to the Eleven Half-Circle. Miranda will be wonderin' what's become of us.'

When they arrived at the ranch they found Miranda waiting anxiously on the veranda. As they dismounted she ran to her father.

'I was worried,' she said. 'I expected you back earlier.'

'Well, we're back now,' Coolidge replied. 'Sure could use some coffee.' She turned with an anxious look to Bendix.

'Are you all right, Mr Bendix?

Remember you are just recovering from a head wound.'

'Sure, I'm fine now. Thanks to you,' Bendix replied.

'Come inside', she said.

They made their way inside the ranch house and soon Miranda appeared with a pot of coffee.

'This is good,' Coolidge said, 'but tell the cook to rustle up somethin' more substantial. Reckon we could all do with some good hot chowder.'

While they were eating there was a clatter of hoofs in the yard, then the marshal entered. He looked grave.

'What's the problem?' Coolidge asked.

The marshal looked at Jennings. 'Got a telegram this morning,' he said. 'It's from a man called Morris.'

'Morris?' Jennings said. 'That's my deputy. I left him in charge of things back at Driftwood.'

'Well, looks like he could do with some assistance. Seems like things have got rough up there and are threatenin' to get out of hand.'

'What do you mean?'

'I guess there wasn't time for details. Looks like he's got his hands full with a gang of desperadoes threatenin' to tear the town apart. Wants to know if you can get back.'

'Hell,' Jennings said, 'That's just what I was afraid of.' He turned to Bendix. 'I figured things would be OK if I left. Remember I was worried that Driftwood could become a bloodbath if I stayed? Well, looks like I was right, only it's happenin' anyway.'

'You'd better get back,' Coolidge said. 'Don't worry, I can handle the Rocking-Horse.'

Jennings turned to Bendix. 'You stay. I'll head for Driftwood.'

Bendix was thinking fast, but even so he couldn't help but notice the anxious look in Miranda's eyes.

'We don't know for sure that this has anything to do with the Presidio Kid tie-up,' Jennings continued. 'It could be something altogether different from the trouble we had with those coyotes in the saloon.'

'I don't think so,' Bendix replied. 'After all, how were things in Driftwood before those *hombres* arrived with the Rocking-Horse brand on their horses?'

Jennings nodded.

'I see what you mean. Things have been quiet for a long time. It would be too much of a coincidence if there wasn't a connection.'

'Can't Morris handle this himself?' Bendix said.

'The telegraph message says not,' Jennings replied.

Marshal Mercer had been listening with attention to the conversation. Now he intervened.

'You made mention of the Presidio Kid,' he said. 'He ain't been active in a long time. Perhaps you'd better explain to me how he got into the picture.'

Briefly Bendix updated him on some of the details surrounding Gilpin. The marshal looked thoughtful but did not refer to the matter when Bendix had finished. Instead he turned to Coolidge.

'I'm on my way to see Luke Grey,' he said. 'Perhaps while Mr Jennings and Mr Bendix are coming to a decision, you'd care to accompany me to the Tumbling W?'

Coolidge finished his mug of coffee. 'Sure would,' he said. He turned to Bendix. 'I'll leave you boys to decide what you plan to do. Please don't feel any obligation to the Eleven Half-Circle, but whatever decision you come to you know you are both more than welcome here.'

He got to his feet and together he and the marshal went to the door. Turning back, he said:

'Miranda, look after our guests and let them have any supplies they might need.'

When he had gone and they had eaten the last of the breakfast, Bendix and Jennings excused themselves and went outside. Avoiding the bunkhouse, they began to walk away till, reaching the top of a slight incline behind the corral, they stopped and looked back at the ranch.

'A mighty nice fella, Coolidge,' Jennings said inconsequentially. 'And that Miranda sure is some woman.'

Bendix gave him a puzzled look, not understanding his meaning.

'Seems to me it sure would be a pity for you to leave right now,' Jennings added.

'I thought that's what we were discussin',' Bendix said. He hesitated for a moment. 'How about you? Wouldn't it be a pity for you to leave too?'

'What do you mean?'

'Oh, nothin' much, I guess.'

'Go on, there's somethin' eatin' you.'

'It's just that I sometimes wondered whether you had more of a stake in all this than you let on. You were ready enough to quit Driftwood and come ridin' down here.'

Jennings looked out across the range before turning back to Bendix.

'You're right,' he said. 'I guess I should have told you in the first place.

It's no secret. I suppose it's just that I never talked much about it. I do have a bigger stake in all this. You see, my brother was on one of those trains that the Presidio Kid and his gang attacked. He was killed tryin' to fight them off.'

Silence fell between them till Bendix put his hand on Jennings's arm.

'I'm sorry,' he said.

Jennings glanced at him and smiled. 'Anyway,' he said, 'Let's get back to what we were talkin' about. How long is it since we left to come down here?'

'I don't know. A while. What's that got to do with anythin'?'

'Think for a moment and then answer this question. Just what are those owlhoots doin' still hangin' about Driftwood? Even if they're just a few cowpunchers on the prod, shouldn't they all be back here now, same as us? We figured we might have trouble with them on our tail but apart from one incident it hasn't materialized.'

'I think I see what you're getting at.

You got a point. So just exactly what are you sayin'?'

'I'm sayin' there's still a tie-up between what's happenin' down here and what's goin' on in Driftwood. And that means there's still a link to your old cabin in the hills. I got a feelin' that whatever the answer to this Presidio Kid caper is, it's goin' to lead back there in some way.'

Bendix was quiet. He scratched his chin and looked at Jennings for some moments.

'Hell,' he said, 'I just can't figure this. I guess I ain't got the logic of you lawmen. But I think I get your drift.'

'We're workin' in the dark but I reckon it's pretty clear what we ought to do now. Leavin' aside what Morris says, it makes sense to have one of us handlin' things at this end and one of us on hand at the other end.'

'Maybe you're right. I just don't know. Are you sure you'll be OK to deal with things in Driftwood?'

Jennings laughed. 'I been marshal

there a long time. Besides, I've got Morris for back-up.' Bendix had seen the marshal in action. He didn't have any worries. 'OK,' he said. 'If you're sure about it. I suggest you take up Coolidge's offer and pick yourself a good horse. I'll ride with you as far as Horse Bend and pick up the steeldust.'

They looked each other in the eye and both smiled.

'You know,' Jennings said, 'at times I almost doubt that the Presidio Kid ever existed.'

'You got the dodger on Gilpin,' Bendix said.

'Yeah, there's always that.'

Neither mentioned Jennings's brother as they made their way to the corral.

After leaving the Eleven Half-Circle, Marshal Mercer and Coolidge rode for the Tumbling W.

'What do you intend doin' when we get there?' Coolidge asked.

The marshal told Coolidge about his meeting with Drake Jordan.

'I don't trust that man,' Coolidge said.

'He wouldn't say how much Miss Otilie is offerin' for the Tumbling W.'

'I can make a guess,' Coolidge said. 'Probably the same as she offered me.'

He named a figure. The marshal whistled.

'Surely that's way less than the property is worth?' he said.

'Sure is. But I wouldn't sell out, no matter what the price.'

'I wouldn't have expected Grey to sell out either,' the marshal said. 'Makes me wonder whether the Rocking-Horse has been applyin' pressure, same as they did to Miranda.'

'That may have been just wild talk on the part of Barrett,' Coolidge replied. 'Miss Otilie may have known nothin' about it.'

'Has there been any pressure to sell?' Mercer asked.

Coolidge shook his head. 'Not so far,' he replied. 'Leastways, not on me.'

'One other thing puzzles me,' the marshal said. 'Where is Miss Otilie getting the cash?'

'It's a big spread. She has interests in town. She must be quite a rich lady.'

'Yeah, maybe so. But where did she get the money for the Rocking-Horse in the first place?'

They rode a little further before the marshal turned to Coolidge.

'You know the stage was robbed?'

Coolidge looked surprised. 'When did that happen?'

'Few days ago.'

'Any idea who did it?'

'Nope, but I'm wonderin' if there could be a connection.'

'How do you mean?'

'Well, like I was sayin', where is Miss Otilie getting the money for these takeovers? OK, she's offerin' you both a lot less than the properties are worth, but they're still tidy sums.'

They rode in silence while Coolidge absorbed what the marshal had said. As they were approaching the Tumbling W he drew his horse to a halt. The marshal did likewise and came up close to him.

'By Jiminy,' said Coolidge, 'you ain't

suggestin' that Miss Otilie is mixed up in the stagecoach robbery?'

The marshal was some time in replying.

'Seb,' he said, 'I just don't know what to think. But I ain't rulin' anything out.'

'Well, I would find that hard to believe. But Miss Otilie has some unsavoury *hombres* on her payroll. I wouldn't put it past some of those gentlemen to be involved in somethin' like that.'

'Let's get goin',' Mercer replied. 'We're nearly at the Tumbling W.'

Mercer had been expecting Luke Grey to meet them when they rode into the yard but, contrary to custom, nobody appeared on the veranda. The two men tied their horses to the hitching post, then stepped up and knocked on the door.

'Place seems a little quiet,' Mercer remarked.

They looked about. There were no signs of activity and little noise apart from the occasional blowing of a horse.

Mercer knocked again and this time, after a pause, the door was opened by a small, slim man Coolidge recognized as Pete Dawkins, the cook.

'We'd like to have a word with Luke Grey,' the marshal said.

Dawkins looked uncertain and anxious. It seemed to take him a few moments to consider the marshal's request before he arrived at a decision.

'Mr Grey isn't well,' he said. 'He don't want no visitors.'

Mercer looked closely at the little man. 'What's this all about?' he said.

After another moment of hesitation the cook opened the door wide. 'You'd better come in,' he said.

Mercer and Coolidge entered the room. The house seemed unusually quiet.

'Mr Grey is resting,' Dawkins said. 'I don't think he would appreciate being disturbed.'

'Resting!' the marshal exclaimed. 'I've known Luke Grey for years and he ain't the type to want a rest in the middle of the day.' He glanced up at a closed door leading to a bedroom. 'Is he in there?'

The cook nodded. Ignoring what he had said, Mercer stepped across the room and knocked on the door. There was no reply so he knocked again. This time a faint voice replied:

'I thought I said I didn't want any disturbance.'

'Luke, it's Marshal Mercer and Seb Coolidge.'

There was no reply.

'We're comin' in,' the marshal said, and turned the door handle. He had been expecting the door to be locked but it opened and he went into the bedroom, followed by Coolidge. Luke Grey was lying in bed. The marshal gasped as his eyes adjusted and he saw the state the man was in. His face was swollen and bruised; one eye was closed and there were lacerations to his cheeks and lips.

'Hell, what happened to you?' the marshal exclaimed.

There was no reply. Dawkins's voice sounded behind the marshal, apologizing for not keeping them out. Coolidge had strided to the opposite side of the bed and pulled up a straight-backed chair.

'Luke,' he said, 'I don't know who did this to you, but you can be sure he's goin' to pay.'

Luke Grey's head moved slightly on the pillow. Through his bloodshot good eye he looked at his fellow-rancher.

'Wouldn't do no good,' he murmured.

'Take it easy,' the marshal said, 'but try and tell us what happened.'

He turned to the cook.

'Fetch him a drink,' he said.

When Grey had had a sip of cold water, he began to speak in low tones.

'Bushwhacked,' he said. 'I never saw who did it.'

'How many of 'em?'

'Not sure. More than one.'

'Where? When?'

'Don't know. What day is it now?

Down by Horse Creek.'

The creek ran through Tumbling W land before continuing to form a loop round the town which gave it its name.

'Here? On your own property?'

'On the way back from town.'

On a sudden inspiration Mercer asked: 'Don't tell me. On the way back from seein' Drake Jordan?'

A hint of surprise showed on the rancher's battered face. 'How did you know?'

'Just a guess.'

Coolidge looked across the bed at Mercer. 'What did you want with Jordan?'

Grey's head moved again on the pillow. 'It don't matter,' he mumbled.

The cook was hovering near by. 'I think Mr Grey is exhausted,' he said. 'Perhaps you'd better leave him for now.'

Mercer nodded. 'Yeah, I guess you're right.'

He got to his feet, touched Grey lightly on the shoulder, and left the room. When the bedroom door had closed the cook turned to the marshal.

'He's taken a bad beating,' he said. 'It's not just his face.'

'Has the doctor been out to see him?'

'No. Mr Grey said he didn't want no one else involved.'

'Never mind that. I'll arrange for Doc Steiger to come over as quickly as possible.'

'The place seems very quiet,' Coolidge said. 'Where are the ranch-hands?' The cook looked shifty.

'It's round-up,' he replied. 'They're out on the range.'

'We never saw anyone as we rode in here.'

There was a silence before the cook spoke again.

'A few of them are out on the range. Others have left. I guess they didn't want no trouble.'

'Didn't take them long,' Mercer snarled. He felt a sudden respect for the little cook. 'At least you didn't run out on him,' he said.

The marshal and Coolidge stepped into leather and rode away, heading for Horse Bend.

'You reckon the Rocking-Horse is behind this too?' Coolidge asked.

'Looks like it,' the marshal said. 'I reckon Grey was bein' pressed to accept the Rocking-Horse offer. The papers were probably drawn up pronto. He was in Horse Bend seein' Jordan in order to make clear he wasn't signin' nothin'.'

'And then he got dry-gulched and changed his mind?'

'Or they held his hand while he signed the papers.' The marshal turned to Coolidge. 'If I'm right about this,' he said, 'I guess you can count yourself lucky the same pressure ain't been applied to you. But I reckon you're next.'

Coolidge looked grim, thinking of what had happened to Miranda.

'You go on to Horse Bend,' he said. 'I'd better get back to the Eleven Half-Circle.'

The marshal nodded. 'I'll stop by later,' he said.

★　★　★

When Bendix had seen Jennings off he decided to have a look around town before collecting the steeldust. There was nothing remarkable about the place, just the usual sprawl of false-fronted clapboard buildings and a scattering of adobe shacks. The only larger building was the one that passed as a hotel, the Sand Bar, which stood a couple of doors from the bank and the general store, opposite to which was the restaurant. Remembering his conversation with the waitress, Bendix decided to drop by the restaurant on the chance of picking up any further information that might prove useful. As he came through the door she looked up and smiled in recognition. The place was quiet and he again took a seat by the window from which he had a view over the street.

'Hello,' she said, coming up to him. 'I've been worried about you.' Not understanding at first what she meant, he gave her an enquiring look.

'I saw them take you away in the buckboard,' she said. 'I wasn't sure how badly hurt you were.'

Bendix smiled. 'Just a graze,' he said. 'It weren't anything.'

'Those two deserved everything they got,' she said admiringly. 'Somebody should have stood up to them a long time ago. What can I get you? It's on the house.'

'Just coffee,' Bendix replied.

She moved away and was quickly back with the coffee and some biscuits.

'Have you got a moment?' Bendix asked as she poured the steaming black liquid.

'Sure.' She pulled up a chair. Bendix poured a mug of coffee and offered one to her but she shook her head.

'Those two *hombres*,' Bendix began. 'You told me they rode for the Rocking-Horse. What do you know

126

about the woman who runs it?'

'Miss Otilie? Don't see much of her. She used to come into town from time to time but that was a long time ago. Some folks say it's because she got scarred up. Feels embarrassed about it.'

'Scarred up?'

'Seems she was in some sort of accident. I only seen it once. All down her cheek. She wore a kind of veil but I still noticed it.'

'How long has she been the owner of the Rocking-Horse?'

'She became the owner about two, three years ago. Built it up since.'

Bendix paused for thought. 'I suppose, things bein' the way they are, she don't take kindly to visitors?' he said after a moment or two.

'Like I said, she keeps herself to herself. The only people I know who've been out to the Rocking-Horse are the marshal and Doc Steiger.'

'Thanks,' Bendix said.

She hesitated for a moment before standing up.

'How is Miss Miranda?' she said, 'if you don't mind me askin'. Must have been mighty upsettin' for her.'

'Miss Miranda? Oh, she's fine.'

'She's a real nice lady. Calls in now and again.'

'I'll tell her you were askin' after her.'

The waitress moved off and after finishing his coffee Bendix got to his feet.

'Can you direct me towards Doctor Steiger's place?' he asked.

The waitress accompanied him to the door and pointed down the street.

'Take the first turn to the left,' she said. 'It ain't far.'

As he walked away her eyes followed him. Why had he been asking questions? Come to think of it, what was he doing in Horse Bend in the first place? It was strange, but she somehow felt more comfortable that he was there.

It was easy to find the doctor's house, especially as the doctor was sitting outside on the veranda smoking a pipe. He looked up at Bendix's approach, recognizing him.

'Isn't it Mr Bendix?' he said. 'How is that head wound?'

'You done a good job,' Bendix replied. 'Appreciate it. Let me know what I owe you.'

Appearing to ignore his last remark, the doctor continued: 'And the Eleven Half-Circle?'

'Fine so far as I'm aware.'

The doctor beckoned to a chair. 'Guess you got a purpose in comin' out here. Let me get you a drink.'

He went inside and reappeared with a bottle of bourbon and a couple of glasses. When he had poured he looked at Bendix.

'Well, what can I do for you?'

Bendix took a long swallow of the whiskey. 'It's actually about Miss Otilie Stevens.'

The doctor didn't reply.

'I must confess to an interest in that lady,' Bendix continued, 'which is not altogether connected with the unfortunate incident involving Miss Coolidge. I hope you don't mind me asking, but I understand Miss Otilie once received some sort of injury and that you were the person who treated it.'

It was the doctor's turn to drink, following which he put his pipe to his mouth and drew deeply upon it.

'Before I respond to your question,' he said, 'perhaps you could tell me what is the nature of your interest in Miss Otilie? If you don't mind me saying so, I know nothing at all about you or your friend — Mr Jennings, was it?'

'Sure,' Bendix replied. 'I can quite see how our sudden appearance and my interest in the Rocking-Horse might appear questionable. Let me give you a little of the background.'

Once again he gave a brief account of what had happened to bring him and Jennings to Horse Bend. When he had finished the doctor laid aside his pipe and looked across the lawn and between the houses to where he could see the cottonwood trees lining the banks of Horse Creek.

'OK,' he said. 'Obviously I am professionally bound not to disclose too much information, but I can confirm what you say. You understand this all happened some time ago.'

'Two years?' Bendix intervened.

'Slightly more, if I remember aright. I received an urgent call to visit Miss Otilie as she had received a wound. I did my duty and tended to her.'

'Might I ask what your diagnosis was?'

The doctor thought for a moment, drawing on his pipe as he did so.

'I don't see why not. Miss Otilie had received burns to the face and to the right shoulder. There was other scarring but those were the main wounds.'

'Any idea how she got them?'

'She said that a gas lamp had exploded. I wasn't concerned to delve too closely into the reasons. My concern was with the welfare of my patient.'

He paused as if reminiscing. 'Funny, isn't it,' he said, 'that we both subsequently ended up in a place like Horse Bend.'

Bendix gave a start. 'Didn't this happen at the Rocking-Horse?' he said.

'Why, no. That's what I mean about it being strange. These events occurred before she bought the Rocking-Horse and before I moved to Horse Bend.'

'So where did it happen? Where was it you tended to her injuries?'

'She was living in Presidio then,' the doctor replied.

'Presidio!'

'Sure. And that's another strange thing. The place I visited was a little house on the edge of town. It didn't amount to a shuck. And yet not long after she was the owner of the Rocking-Horse.' He turned to Bendix. 'I'm afraid that's about all I can tell you. Hope it's been of some help.'

'Thanks, doctor. I really appreciate you givin' me this information.' The doctor regarded Bendix with a quizzical expression. 'You know,' he said, 'seems to me you're missin' somethin' pretty obvious.'

'Oh, what's that?'

'Well, if I've understood you correctly, you got involved with this affair, whatever it is, because you think you might have been mistaken for somebody else, for this man . . . what was his name?'

'Gilpin,' Bendix replied.

'Yes, Gilpin. If that's the case, why don't you carry on being Gilpin? Apparently none of these people who were lookin' for him know any different. If you carry on as Gilpin, maybe that way you would draw the Presidio Kid, or whoever it is you think is involved, to you? It might be an easy way to get to the bottom of the matter.'

Bendix's brows contracted in thought.

'Yes, perhaps you're right,' he said. 'In fact, now that you mention it, I think it's something I've had at the back of my mind for a while. Maybe the time has come to let the word spread that Ed Gilpin is in Horse Bend.'

After thanking the doctor once more he finished his drink and got to his feet.

The doctor walked with him down the garden path.

'Of course,' he said, 'this idea of you taking on the mantle of Gilpin might have some leverage. On the other hand it could be a sure fire way to get yourself killed.'

Bendix turned to the grey-haired oldster.

'Yeah,' he said. 'The thought had occurred to me.'

5

Midway between Long Bucket and Cedar Slide the railroad passes through a scene of red-granite buttes with steep canyons. Stunted pine trees cling to the ridges and great masses of rock are heaped in piles alongside the track. It was mid-afternoon and a train was panting along the upgrade, drawn by two toiling engines. From the cover of huge boulders the Presidio Kid and a group of mean-looking gunhawks were watching its slow progress. They had their bandannas pulled up and the Kid was wearing a long black mask.

'This is goin' to be easy,' one of them remarked. 'If'n the train gets much slower it'll just grind to a halt.'

'Hell, I could crawl faster,' one of his companions replied.

The Presidio Kid laughed and spoke in a curiously high-pitched voice.

'That's why I chose this spot. Now quit talkin' and get ready.'

Soon further conversation was almost impossible as the roar of the engines grew louder, reverberating from the walls of the canyon like a cannonade. Black smoke billowed from the smoke-stacks and clouds of steam hissed and boiled as the train laboured up the long slope. When it was almost alongside the hidden horsemen they rode out of cover, firing as they did so. The driver reached for a rifle but a shot took him in the shoulder and he reeled away. Coming alongside, a couple of the horsemen swung themselves into the cabin. Further back there was firing coming from the baggage car where the baggage master and a guard had their weapons but they had been lazing; not expecting any trouble, they were caught by surprise. Their shots flew harmlessly overhead and riding up to the carriage, the Presidio Kid flung a stick of dynamite through the open door. The guard jumped from the train but fell straight into the path of one of the galloping owlhoots. His scream of pain was cancelled as the dynamite exploded and the baggage car went up in a sheet of flame.

The train was still moving but almost imperceptibly and even now a lot of the passengers in the other cars were unaware of what was happening. As the train lurched they began to realize that something was wrong. Some of them started to shout and cry while others poked their heads though the windows. Some sporadic shots broke out from the rear car and a man appeared on the platform, blazing away with a rifle. As the riders approached he swung down, seeking cover behind the train, but before he could dodge round the corner he was hit by a number of shots. He slumped dead on the tracks. Behind him the conductor appeared with one of the brakemen and as a couple of the outlaws hauled themselves over the rail, a tussle took place. One of the gunmen was lifted bodily and thrown over but there was no escape for the defenders from the blaze of lead which sent them spinning to the floor.

It was all over. The outlaws were in control of the train and as the passengers huddled together they patrolled the cars while the Presidio Kid set up to blow the safe.

'Keep your heads down!'

The passengers bent forward, covering their ears, then there came a second explosion. Women and children howled in fear and some of the male passengers gritted their teeth. There was nothing they could do. The front end of the train was filled with smoke and through the haze and the stench the owlhoots were emptying the safe of its contents. Some of the outlaws were shouting and laughing and one of them was firing his gun into the air. Presently they climbed down from the train and mounted their horses. The passengers watched with a mixture of shock and relief as the gang wheeled their mounts and began riding away down the canyon. At their rear rode a black-clad and masked figure. Pulling hard on the reins of a big buckskin so that it reared into the air, its rider called back to the badly damaged train and its battered occupants:

'Tell them it was the Presidio Kid!'

Then with a whoop, the Kid rode off. Slowly the bemused passengers began to move about, some seeking comfort, others trying to ascertain the extent of the damage and bring succour to the wounded. Some of them were too dazed to take in what had happened. It seemed unreal, like something out of a nightmare. Vaguely, one or two of them began to remember incidents which had happened in the past.

'The Presidio Kid,' one of them mused. 'I thought the Presidio Kid had gone to ground a long time ago.'

'Figured he must be in jail, if I thought about it at all.'

'Well, if he was in jail he must have busted loose because it sure looks like he's back.'

It was late in the afternoon when Bendix left the doctor and made his way to the livery stable to collect the steeldust. As he rode out of town he was thinking about the doctor's suggestion and the best way to make it known that he was Ed Gilpin. Once the story was put around, he wasn't sure what to expect but the trail which had led him to Horse Bend seemed to have gone cold.

What were the facts? Ed Gilpin had ridden with the Presidio Kid. He had dropped out of sight. His whereabouts had become known, triggering off a series of events in which Bendix had got caught up and as a consequence of which he had been shot. The knee still troubled him. There was a connection to the Rocking-Horse and things were happening both in Horse Bend and Driftwood. Those places were a considerable way apart, so it seemed that something important was involved. Why had Gilpin hidden himself away? Was there something he knew which involved the Presidio Kid? Did he have some information? Or had he riled the Presidio Kid and his gang to such an extent that even after all this time they wanted revenge?

Whatever the answer, he would be putting himself on the line by posing as Gilpin — at least till someone realized the charade; in which case he might become even more of a target.

Evening was drawing down and shadows were creeping across the range. Ahead of him a rising section of ground covered with low brush held the sun's late glow and there was a stillness about the land. Bendix suddenly felt good, allowing his troubled thoughts to subside for a few moments as he enjoyed the peace and tranquillity, the beauty of the scene, and the strength of the steeldust between his legs. The air was cool after the heat of the day and carried the scent of sage.

As he worked his way along the side

of the hill Bendix paused to take in the view. At the same moment there came a crump of air and Bendix felt the passage of a bullet as a shot boomed out from the hillside. He threw himself flat along the back of the horse and dug in his spurs. The steeldust burst forward. Another shot rang out and whined overhead. Bendix touched the reins lightly and the horse instantly changed direction. The steeldust was a good peg horse and trained for speed. It was all Bendix could do to hang on as the horse veered again and went charging along at break-neck speed.

Soon Bendix reckoned he was out of danger but he wasn't about to let the matter go. Someone had tried to dry-gulch him and he didn't intend to let him get away with it. Who could it be? One of the Rocking-Horse hands out for revenge for what had happened to Barrett?

Bendix brought the steeldust to a halt and began to work his way back around the hill. He figured that whoever had shot at him would probably have ridden off towards town, in the opposite direction to the one Bendix had taken. If he moved quickly, he might be able to circle ahead of him and maybe catch him as he approached Horse Bend.

The slope of the hill cut Bendix off from any view of the trail he had ridden but as he climbed higher and came round the angle of the hill he saw a rider below him, moving quickly towards town. Touching the flanks of the horse lightly with his spurs, Bendix set off in pursuit.

Darkness had descended and Bendix was concealed from the rider's sight not only because of his elevated position, but also by the covering brush. Although it meant that at times he could no longer see the rider, Bendix kept just below the brow of the hill in order to avoid being skylined.

The steeldust sped quickly over the ground and Bendix reckoned he was making good ground on his assailant. Whoever it was had not gained much of a start; by the time he had reached his horse Bendix had already turned back and was on his tail. The slope of the hill was gradually diminishing and Bendix wanted one more look at the rider before he made an all-out effort to get ahead of him.

Riding down the slope a little, he saw his target down below. Bendix was not far behind and he calculated that if he pushed the steeldust hard he could emerge on the lower trail ahead of him within the next two or three miles. The steeldust responded to his gentle touch, bounding across the terrain as if it felt the need to extend its muscles and sinews after having been cooped up at the livery stables.

The hill had levelled out now and in a short distance Bendix would be out of cover and into the open. He had a pretty good memory of the terrain, however. That was something he had learned to do at an early age, when he realized how important it could be in giving him an edge. There was a little clump of bushes he had in mind not too far out of town and he spurred the horse to even greater efforts as he aimed towards it. He was back on the trail but he could not see the other rider. He glanced back over his shoulder but there was no sign of him. The trail took a bend and before long he could see the bushes ahead of him.

Pulling on the reins he slowed the horse and rode into cover. Quickly he undid his lariat. No sooner had he done so than he heard the clattering of hoofs back along the trail. Watching intently through the screening bushes, he held the lariat at shoulder height on his left side. As the rider came by he whirled the rope to the right and over his head. The man suddenly turned but before he realized what was happening the loop landed over his shoulders with the honda sliding down the rope, taking up the slack as it went. As the horse galloped on the rider was plucked from the saddle and came crashing to the ground. Bendix secured the rope to his saddle horn, jumped down from the steeldust and dragged the roped gun-slick to his feet. The man was badly shaken. His clothes were torn and blood was seeping from a grazed cheek. Leaning over, Bendix undid the man's gunbelt and threw it to one side.

'You'd better start talkin',' Bendix snapped.

The fall had winded the owlhoot and he was gasping for breath.

'Well?' Bendix said.

'I don't know what the hell this is about,' the man stuttered.

'You know what it's about. You tried to dry-gulch me. I want to know why.'

'You must be mistaken. You must have got the wrong man.'

Bendix drew the Smith & Wesson from his holster. 'I ain't got time for foolin',' he rapped. 'For the last time, start talkin'.' He drew the rope tight and drew back the hammer of the gun.

'All right,' the man said. 'I'll talk, but let me out of this first.'

'Talk first, then I might consider

lettin' you loose.'

The man looked at Bendix and saw something in his expression which broke any further resistance.

'OK, OK,' he began. 'I admit it, I took a shot at you but it was only meant as a warnin'. I didn't intend killin' you.'

'A warnin'? What sort of a warnin'?'

The man was searching for the right words, the words he hoped might soften whatever punishment was coming his way, but his very hesitation was a giveaway.

'Let me tell you what I think,' Bendix said. 'I think you were out to gain a little glory for yourself by gettin' rid of me.'

'Why would I do that? I don't know you.'

'You know Barrett. I would guess he's a friend of yours.'

'Barrett? I don't know anyone name of Barrett.'

Bendix strode a little way down the trail to where the man's horse had drawn up. Sure enough it bore the

Rocking-Horse brand.

'OK,' the man said, 'so I ride for the Rocking-Horse. That don't mean to say — '

Before he could go any further Bendix stopped him. 'Look,' he said, 'I've had enough of this charade. I know what you were doin'. The only thing I'm not sure about is whether you were actin' on your own or on behalf of the Rocking-Horse. Either way, this is what you can do. You can start walkin' away from here and when you get back to the Rocking-Horse you can tell Miss Otilie Stevens that Ed Gilpin is in town.'

'Gilpin?' the man repeated.

'Yeah. I have a hunch she'll know who I am and I reckon she might appreciate knowin' I'm around.'

The man looked bewildered.

'You don't need to know nothin' more,' Bendix said. 'Just make sure Miss Otilie gets the message.'

He put his gun back into its holster and quickly released the man from his entanglement with the lariat.

'Take your boots off,' he snapped.

'My boots? What do you mean?'

'Take 'em off and then start walkin'. You're lucky it ain't too far to town.'

'Hell, it's a rough road. What about my hoss?'

'I'll see to the horse. Now get movin' before I start to lose patience.'

The man looked as though he was about to expostulate again but thought better of it. Still grumbling, he commenced to shuffle his way down the dusty track. Bendix watched him for a while before picking up the man's gunbelt. Leading the man's horse behind him, he rode the steeldust in the opposite direction towards the Eleven Half-Circle.

★ ★ ★

Coolidge was a worried man. He had seen the state that Luke Grey had been left in. Taking that together with the incident involving his daughter at Horse

Bend, he was concerned for the future of the ranch. More than that, he was worried about Miranda. Once again he had reason to feel thankful for Bendix's intervention and when Bendix rode into the yard he called him over to the ranch house. Over a couple of stiff drinks he told Bendix about what had happened to his friend at the Tumbling W and also something of what the marshal had said about his visit to the lawyer.

'Someone tried to dry-gulch me on the way back from town,' Bendix said. 'He was from the Rocking-Horse.'

'I think the time has come to take precautionary measures,' Coolidge replied. 'Seems like that was no idle threat Barrett was makin'.'

'I think you're right,' Bendix said. 'There seems to be a whole stack of evidence buildin' up against the Rocking-Horse.'

Coolidge stroked his chin. 'The marshal was wonderin' where Miss Otilie has acquired the cash to buy the

Tumbling W, or this place for that matter. He mentioned that the stage had been held up. He didn't exactly make a direct accusation, but he seemed to think it was somethin' of a coincidence. I must say, in the light of what has been happenin', that I'm beginnin' to agree.'

'The stage!' Bendix exclaimed. 'Didn't that use to be the prerogative of the Presidio Kid?'

Coolidge gave him a long hard glance. 'That was some time ago,' he said.

'The Presidio Kid disappeared,' Bendix replied. 'Nobody knows what became of him. He could be still around. Somethin' could have happened to start him up again.'

'The same thing that dragged you into it?' Coolidge replied. 'A week ago I would have said it was too fanciful, too far-fetched. Now I'm beginnin' to believe it.'

'There's one way to maybe flush him out, assumin' he's around.'

Bendix told Coolidge about posing as Gilpin and about telling the man who had waylaid him to spread the news that Gilpin was in town. The other blew gently through pursed lips.

'You could be puttin' yourself into a lot of danger. Maybe we should just get together with Mercer and pay a visit to the Rocking-Horse.'

'It might come to that,' Bendix replied, 'but the time's not right. What good would it do? There's got to be some link between the Presidio Kid and the Rocking-Horse, but if we go blusterin' in just now we'd blow the whole shebang. If the Presidio Kid is back on the scene, he'll be alerted. Better for the moment to play things down. Let me see if I can unearth anythin'. And in the meantime, I agree with you that it would be a good idea to prepare for trouble. I take it you've got some reliable men riding for you?'

'They're good men, people I've known for a long time and loyal to the brand.'

Bendix hesitated before speaking again. 'That's probably what Luke Grey thought,' he said.

Coolidge looked at Bendix hard. 'I can't vouch for the Tumbling W,' he said. 'But the Eleven Half-Circle is solid. I'd trust my men with my life.'

'You might need to do just that,' Bendix answered. 'And they might need to prove it.'

They finished their drinks and moved towards the door. It was a beautiful evening. They stood for a few moments on the veranda, then Bendix had a sudden anxious thought.

'Where is Miranda?' he said.

Coolidge pointed to a trail which led behind the corral over pasture lands where some of the horses were grazing. In the distance the figure of his daughter could be seen walking towards the ranch.

'I know what you're thinkin',' Coolidge said, 'and I agree. Now that things have developed the way they have, Miranda needs to be reminded to take care.'

Bendix was surprised at how concerned he had felt about the rancher's daughter.

'It might be a good idea,' he said. 'Especially after what happened with Barrett.'

'The boys keep an eye out for her,' Coolidge said. 'Some of the older hands have known her since she was a child. Besides, she can take care of herself.'

'Still, it's only sensible not to take any chances. If the Rocking-Horse is inclined to apply pressure on you to sell the Eleven Half-Circle, targeting her could be one way to do it.'

Coolidge gave him a knowing look. 'Well,' he said, 'there she is. Why don't you go and tell her yourself?' Bendix hesitated for just a moment before stepping off the veranda.

'Take your time,' the rancher said. 'It's a lovely evening.'

Bendix started to walk. He circled round the corral, jumped a low fence and cut across the pasture, intending to cross Miranda's path. Looking up, he couldn't see her and a surge of something like panic attacked him. A moment later she emerged round a corner of the path and he sighed almost audibly with relief. He was surprised at his reactions. Did she mean more to him than he realized? It was such a short time since he had met her. There surely hadn't been enough time for him to develop any feelings? But there it was. He couldn't deny either the anxiety or the relief.

Striding purposefully forward, he waved his hat, but she must have been looking elsewhere and didn't respond. Then a turn in the path led her away from him until she turned once more and saw him. Waving her arms, she began to move faster and soon their paths intersected and they met. Suddenly Bendix felt awkward. He had been so pleased to see her and so keen to meet up with her that he hadn't considered what he was going to say. He needn't have worried, though, because, taking the initiative, she smiled and said:

'Mr Bendix. What a nice surprise.'

'I was standing on the veranda with your father. We saw you coming down the trail.'

'And you decided to come and meet me? That's nice. And now you're here, let us stroll together. I love walking almost as much as I do riding. What about you, Mr Bendix? Perhaps you don't get the time to simply enjoy the view. I was born here and yet I never grow tired of the country. Look, isn't it a splendid sight?'

Bendix had been more concerned with the way she looked than the surrounding scenery. She was wearing range gear but it did nothing to hide the lines of her body. On her head was a Stetson held in place by a string. It was simple attire but it suited her. Now Bendix turned away and, following her gaze, looked across the fields and the grazing lands to the rolling ridges beyond. Turning his head a little, he could see the faraway blue haze of more distant hills.

'Yeah,' he said. 'It's a fine country.'

They walked a little further and then she turned to him again.

'If you don't mind me saying,' she said, 'but you seem to have a slight limp? I hadn't noticed it before. I hope it's got nothing to do with that horrible Barrett affair.'

Bendix had grown used to the damage to his knee. It caused him occasional pain but he hadn't been aware that he favoured one leg over the other.

'No,' he said. 'It was somethin' else altogether.'

'Well, you must learn to look after yourself. I . . . ' She paused and Bendix faced her.

'Yes,' he prompted.

'I'm sorry,' she replied. 'It was rude of me to say anything.' She looked up at him with her limpid eyes.

'You're lovely,' he said.

Immediately he felt awkward and embarrassed again. She had caught him off his guard and he was afraid he had gone too far.

'I'm sorry,' he murmured, 'I shouldn't have said that.'

She smiled and put her hand on his arm. 'Don't be sorry,' she said. 'I'm not.'

For another moment they stood looking at one another, then he reached up and stroked her hair before drawing her closely to him. She did not resist and for what seemed a long time they leaned together.

'Maybe we'd better continue walking,' he said at length.

Drawing back she looked up at him again.

'Yes,' she said, but did not move. Slowly their faces drew together and their lips touched. When they drew apart they did not continue walking but stood together watching the sun sink lower down the sky as the shadows deepened across the pastures. The sun hung on the lip of the horizon before dropping over the edge.

'You'll go away,' she said at last. 'You don't belong here like I do.'

He didn't reply.

'It doesn't matter,' she said. 'At least you're here now.'

A few faint stars swam into the sky. From a distance they could hear the lowing of the cattle and the cough of a horse.

'I won't go away,' he said. 'Not if you don't want me to.'

She looked up at him, her eyes gleaming.

'I don't want you to,' she whispered.

★ ★ ★

At about the same time Miss Otilie Stevens was standing on the veranda of the Rocking-Horse ranch house, having returned a little earlier from the line cabin. She was feeling animated and on a high, as she always did after one of her escapades. The money from the train robbery was safely stashed away in a safe. Later she would arrange through the lawyer Drake Jordan to have it transferred to the bank without anyone suspecting where it came from.

She breathed in the night air and reflected how things had changed since the whereabouts of Ed Gilpin had come to light. At the time she had had one worry — that the bounty hunter who had unearthed the information might get to him first, but she had not been unduly concerned. She had dispatched riders to seek out the cabin and she had faith that they would get there first and that, in any event, Ed Gilpin could take care of himself.

Her boys had reported back that the cabin was deserted. Where was Gilpin now? As she thought about him she felt a delicious bitter-sweet emotion. Would she see him again? Was he even now on his way? And how would she react if she did see him? What would he think of her now?

She didn't dare pursue her thoughts too far, to even begin to consider that she and Gilpin might get together again and that they might pick things up where they had left them. The Presidio Kid was on the prod again. It was set up for Gilpin to join the outfit. On the other hand, maybe it would have been wiser to let sleeping dogs lie. But she had tried that, she had tried to bury herself on the Rocking-Horse, and it hadn't worked.

Looking up, she saw a rider approaching. A couple of ranch hands appeared from the bunkhouse as he swung down from his horse — a strange one, not bearing the Rocking-Horse brand. He must have hired it from the livery stables.

'Miss Otilie,' he said, seeing her in the shadows of the veranda. 'I got a message for you.'

Miss Otilie stepped forward. Something about the rider's manner coupled with her own thoughts seemed to presage some important announcement, but she tried to show an outward face of calm.

'What message?' she said, and then, looking at him closely, 'Isn't it Daniels? Go ahead, what have you got to say?'

The man addressed as Daniels had

been thinking about how best to explain matters to Miss Otilie. He had a feeling that she might not be too pleased if she knew he had taken a pot shot at the man who had lassoed him and given him the message. He was fairly new to the Rocking-Horse but he felt he had heard the name of Gilpin somewhere. On the walk into Horse Bend he had decided what his story should be. The missing horse was a stumbling block. He had managed to pick up a pair of boots, but his feet hurt.

'It's like this,' he said. 'I was riding to town when my hoss went lame. I left it at the livery stable for the ostler to take care of it. That's why I'm ridin' this old sorrel.'

'I'm not interested in the details,' Miss Otilie said. 'Just get to the point.'

'Well, while the ostler was examinin' the hoss, I went over to the saloon. While I was there, a man approached me. Said he had a message for Miss Otilie. Said his name was Ed Gilpin and that he was in town.'

Miss Otilie's heart gave a thump. If she had not been in the shade of the overhang, Daniels would have seen the way her face blanched.

'Is that all?' she asked, managing to maintain her mask of indifference.

'That's all he said, ma'am.'

'What did he look like, this man?'

'Can't rightly say, ma'am. I'm sorry, but I never took much notice. It all happened pretty quickly.'

'Did he say where he was staying in town?'

'No ma'am, he never said nothin' else. After he gave me the message he just turned round and left.'

'And you didn't follow him? You didn't think the whole thing was a little strange?'

'No, ma'am. I never thought too much of it. Figured the best thing was just to do as the man said and ride back here to let you know.'

Miss Otilie could see that the man was agitated. She had a feeling there was more to his story than he was letting on but she didn't see much point in questioning him further for the moment. She could leave that for later if necessary. Right now she needed to be alone and to think.

'OK,' she said, 'that's fine. You did the right thing to come straight here. Take your horse to the stable and then go the bunkhouse.'

The man shuffled away, leading the sorrel. Miss Otilie watched him go, then turned and went inside the house. The housekeeper, a Mexican woman, was in the kitchen and Miss Otilie called to her to say she was going to her room and was not to be disturbed. When she had closed the bedroom door behind her she lay down on the bed and, looking up at the ceiling, tried to calm herself and consider what she had been told. It seemed almost like fate that she should receive the message at just this time. Maybe things were coming together but she hardly dared to believe it might be so. Then suddenly she sat up and looked at herself in a mirror. Her scarred cheek looked red and angry. She felt tears coming to her eyes, but whether tears of hope or tears of anguish she could not tell.

* * *

Bendix was concerned not to put anybody at the Eleven Half-Circle at further risk, as he feared might happen now that he had issued a challenge by claiming to be Ed Gilpin. At the same time, he wanted to make himself available to anyone who might come to seek him out. His whereabouts would be less easy to find while he was a guest of Seb Coolidge. He was for leaving immediately but Coolidge persuaded him to stay for the rest of the night.

Early next morning, however, he saddled the steeldust to ride to town. He hoped that Miranda was still sleeping, but as he walked the horse out of the yard he glanced up at her room and, although he couldn't be certain, he thought he saw a curtain twitch. He felt a pang almost of guilt. He hadn't said anything to her about moving out of the Eleven Half-Circle. Perhaps he should have discussed things with her but somehow he shrank from the encounter. Her father knew the ramifications of the situation. He could answer her questions. Besides, it would only give her cause for worry, and if things panned out he would be back again soon. And when that happened he didn't intend leaving again. He had told her so much and he knew she would wait for his return.

6

Things were just stirring when Bendix rode into Horse Bend and checked in at the hotel, taking care to spell out his name E. Gilpin in the hotel register. Then he went to the café but the usual waitress was not there. Instead another, older woman served him bacon, egg and beans with the usual strong black coffee.

When he had finished he walked down the street to the marshal's office, but Mercer was not there either. A deputy informed him that he had ridden off not long before, he wasn't sure where. Bendix guessed that he had gone either to the Rocking-Horse or the Tumbling W. He considered whether to pay a visit to the Rocking-Horse himself. He was now convinced that Miss Otilie was deeply involved in whatever was going on but he felt that one more proof was needed, and that proof would be if she made the effort now to contact him in the belief that he was Ed Gilpin.

After strolling around town for a while he returned to the hotel where he had another pot of coffee in the hotel dining room. He wondered what had become of Jennings. Maybe he would wander down to the telegraph office later. When he had finished the coffee he went upstairs to his room but just as he was about to put the key in the lock he hesitated. Something was setting up a warning alarm in his brain. He put his head against the door and listened carefully. He could hear nothing but he was convinced that someone was in the room. He bent down and glanced through the keyhole but all he could see was a stretch of carpet and the leg of a chair. He stood erect again, and began to move noiselessly along the corridor and back down the stairs. The hotel clerk was lounging at his desk. He looked up at Bendix's approach.

'Has anyone been askin' for me?' Bendix asked.

The clerk shook his head.

'Nobody gone up to my room?'

'Not that I know of. I was away from the desk for about ten minutes. I suppose somebody might have gone up durin' that time.'

Bendix turned away and then a thought struck him.

'Who owns this place?' he asked.

Again the clerk shrugged. 'I only work here. I don't ask any questions.'

Bendix had a sudden intuition that the owner of the hotel was Miss Otilie Stevens. Hadn't someone said that in addition to the Rocking-Horse she had a hand in various other enterprises, including owning property in town? He could check on that later. He began walking up the carpeted stairs, drawing his gun as he reached the landing. He walked quickly but noiselessly back to his room, put the key in the lock, then, stepping to one side, pushed the door open. He heard the creak of furniture and he threw himself into the room. Sitting on a chair next to the bed was a thin, dark-haired man with a bushy Mexican-style moustache who looked up at his precipitous arrival.

'Mr Gilpin,' he said. 'I've been expectin' you for some time.'

Bendix's gun was pointed at him but he didn't appear to be perturbed.

'My name is Craven,' he said. 'I act as foreman for Miss Otilie Stevens.'

'What the hell are you doin' here?' Bendix snapped. He had a pretty good idea but he needed to act a role.

'I apologize if I surprised you. I agree it's rather unorthodox.'

Bendix looked towards a door which led on to the balcony. He had left it unlocked and guessed his visitor had come in by that route. If Miss Otilie owned the hotel, he probably had a key anyway.

'Why enter my room this way?' Bendix said. 'What's wrong with knockin'? You're lucky I didn't shoot.'

'I just wanted to make sure I didn't

miss you. I take it you have heard of Miss Otilie Stevens? I have a message from her. She would like to see you.'

Bendix's eyes were scanning the room. Craven had probably been searching it. Why? Miss Otilie must be keen to establish his identity.

'Yeah? Maybe I'm not interested in seein' her.'

'Then why leave a message to that effect?'

Bendix smiled. 'I left a message that I was in town. The rest is down to her.'

'I ain't got time to quibble,' the man said. 'Like I say, Miss Otilie would like to see you. It's up to you. You can ignore the request or you can ride out later. Or you can come now with me. I would advise the last.'

Bendix looked at him. 'Is that a threat?' he said.

The man got to his feet. 'I'm goin' back now,' he said. 'If you want to accompany me, we'll take a walk down to the livery stables.'

Bendix holstered the Smith & Wesson.

'I ain't doin' nothin' else,' he said. 'Let's go.'

They picked up the steeldust and began to ride out of town. As they left the last adobe houses, a couple of riders emerged from an alley and closed in behind them.

'Seems like we got company,' Bendix said.

'All part of the service,' Craven replied.

They continued to ride in silence. Bendix was thinking about his forthcoming meeting with Miss Otilie. What would he say when he met her? He hadn't given it a lot of thought so far. Glancing behind him he took note of the riders who remained just in their rear. They looked a couple of mean *hombres*. He began to think that maybe he had gone about things in the wrong way. Maybe it would have been better to approach the Rocking-Horse with the marshal for backing. They were passing the sign on the edge of Rocking-Horse property.

Rocking-Horse
Sighted for Sharps .50
Shoots today, kills today.

'Not exactly friendly,' Bendix commented.

'Ain't meant to be. Means what it says.'

'Guess I'm lucky to have an invite,' Bendix replied, 'and you boys along to protect me.'

Craven gave him an ugly glance and spat through his front teeth.

'What it says works both ways,' he snarled. 'Comin' and goin'.'

They moved forward once more. Despite the warning sign, the trail was fairly well marked so it came as a surprise to Bendix when after a time they turned off and began to ride in a different direction. He was about to make a comment but then decided against it. He was in it now and there was no backing out. Better just go along with Craven, at least for the time being. One thing helped to reassure him.

Craven had shown no sign that he doubted his identity. He seemed to accept that he was Gilpin.

'How long you been with the Rocking-Horse?' Bendix ventured.

'Long enough,' the man replied.

Bendix was not going to get much out of him. He glanced behind. The other two riders were still there. Presently the scene began to change. It was less grassy and there were low broken hills and draws. Bendix was considering what to do when they came in sight of the line cabin. They rode into the dusty yard and swung down from the leather. Craven knocked on the door. He went inside and presently returned. 'Miss Otilie will see you now,' he said.

Bendix hesitated on the veranda, looking about him, suspecting it might be some sort of trap. Craven's lip curled in a sneer.

'You'll probably have guessed,' he said. 'I got some of the boys out there covering the place. I'll be right here with these two *hombres*. Don't think about pullin' any tricks. Don't try and get clever.'

The man turned and led his horse to a barn behind the cabin, accompanied by the other two riders. Bendix still paused on the veranda, wondering what he was going to find. Then he knocked gently on the door.

'Come in!' a voice rang out.

Bendix stepped through the door. His immediate reaction was one of surprise. He had been unsettled by the fact that they had not ridden to the ranch. Now he was taken aback by the luxury and comfort on display. From the outside the place might look ordinary enough — maybe a little bigger than normal — but inside it was richly furnished with an expensive-looking leather sofa and matching chairs, a thick-piled carpet, bookshelves lined with books, a mahogany table on which stood a lamp, and tasteful fittings. This much Bendix observed in the dim light before his attention was drawn to the figure of a woman seated in a chair in a corner of the room away from the window.

'Miss Otilie?' he said.

The figure rose to its feet and stood in the shadows, seeming reluctant to come forward.

'Mr Gilpin,' she said at length and her voice had an unexpected tremor. Her face was away from him and she made no move towards him. He stood feeling awkward and uncertain. Time seemed to have slowed and she might have been standing in that fashion indefinitely before she slowly turned her head towards him. Her gaze fell on him like a weight till she turned away and he thought he detected something like a sob escape from her lips.

Gathering herself together, she advanced towards him and, as the lamplight fell on the side of her face, he was startled to see how badly scarred was her cheek. She came slowly towards him and he tried to read the expression on her face. It was a strange expression, one he found difficult to read. Standing in front of him, she looked closely into his features.

'You're not Ed Gilpin,' she said.

Bendix hadn't expected to deceive her. His assumption of Gilpin's identity had been a means of confirming her connection to his old friend and of getting to see her. Now he was at a loss how to proceed. If she had been angry he would have known how to react but he could not understand her attitude. It seemed at once to be matter of fact and disillusioned, weary and resigned. Looking into her eyes, he saw sadness and disappointment.

'You're right,' he said. 'I'm not Ed Gilpin. My name is Clugh Bendix. Ed Gilpin was an old friend of mine.'

At his words she seemed to perk up a little. The sadness in her eyes evaporated and a faint glint appeared.

'Clugh Bendix,' she said. 'Yes, I remember the name. Ed used to speak of you quite often.'

She turned and gestured to a chair next to hers. 'Forgive my inattention,' she said. 'You must be tired and thirsty. What can I get you? A whiskey? I can recommend the blend. I have it especially imported.'

'I'd appreciate it,' Bendix replied, struck by the odd way she seemed to take pride in being able to offer him an expensive drink at such an inappropriate moment. He moved to the chair and sat down while she took a bottle from a cabinet and poured two drinks. She came across with them and, bending over, turned up the lamp so that he was able to observe her more closely. From this side she was an attractive woman but when she turned he saw the red blaze of the scar that ran down her cheek. Her hair was dark and cut short and when she looked at him he saw that her eyes were blue. She was wearing a very fashionable and expensive gown of dark-purple velvet and round her neck was a choker of the same material.

'Well, Mr Bendix, I must apologize for the manner in which you were conducted here. You must forgive me.

It's just that when I received your message I was particularly anxious to see you.'

'No,' he replied. 'You must forgive me for misleading you and giving you the impression that I was Ed Gilpin.'

She was silent for a moment as she took a drink and seemed to gather herself for the next question.

'Tell me,' she said. 'Since you are an old friend of Ed Gilpin, what has happened to him? Perhaps you do not know.'

It was Bendix's turn to pause and think before replying. In the end he could see no way of breaking the news gently.

'I'm afraid that Gilpin is dead,' he replied. 'I buried him myself. He was unwell. I looked after him during his final days. I'm sorry. I can see that you and he must have been close.'

'I loved him,' she replied.

Somehow Bendix felt no surprise. She had spoken the words simply and having said them, she seemed to become more relaxed.

'Did he ever speak of me?' she said.

Bendix was trying to remember but he couldn't recall Gilpin ever mentioning her.

'I wasn't called Stevens then,' she said. 'I was called Sandoz, Otilie Sandoz. I'm part Mexican.'

'I'm afraid I don't recall him mentioning either name. He was in quite a bad way when I found him. He didn't have much to say at all.'

'Where was this?' she asked.

'He was living in a cabin in the hills, near a place called Driftwood.'

'Ah,' she said, 'so that much was true.'

'You knew about the cabin?' Bendix said.

'Just lately, yes. I sent some of my boys to trace him. They found the cabin but it was deserted. I thought he must have left — and then you showed up.' She suddenly turned so that Bendix could see her wounded cheek.

'Look,' she said. 'I was beautiful once.'

'You still are,' Bendix said.

Suddenly she laughed. 'That's very nice of you, Mr Bendix. But I'm not fooled.' She started to laugh again, then took a long drink of the whiskey.

'You know,' she continued, 'that's what Ed Gilpin told me, but I knew he was lying too. I knew that things could never be the same again between us when I received this wound. Oh yes, he would have gone along with the lie, but I wanted no man's pity, especially not his. So I sent him away. He wouldn't go, but in the end I sent him away.'

Bendix was beginning to feel uncomfortable. There was an edge to her voice which hadn't been there before.

'How did you meet Gilpin?' she asked.

'We were ridin' for the same brand. That seems a long time ago. We went our separate ways.' Bendix felt that he was getting on to dangerous ground.

'You went your separate ways,' she repeated and laughed again. 'Mr Bendix, have you any idea of just how separate your ways must have become?'

'I'm not sure I know what you mean.'

'I think you do,' she said, 'but let me spell it out for you. You could say that as well as riding with you, Gilpin also rode with me. Maybe you didn't really know your friend Gilpin as well as you thought you did.'

She stopped talking and got to her feet. Bendix watched as she crossed the room and opened the door to the room beyond. In a few moments she was back, holding something in her hand which she tossed in Bendix's direction. He bent down and picked it up off the floor. It was a black satin mask, like a yashmak.

'Doesn't that convince you?' she said. 'You wouldn't be here and you wouldn't be pretending to be someone else if you hadn't already guessed that I am the Presidio Kid.'

Bendix felt an involuntary quickening of surprise but it was only momentary. He realized that he had come to that conclusion, although he had not framed it in so many words.

'So it was true that Gilpin was a wanted man?' he said.

'A wanted man? Oh yes,' she murmured, 'oh yes.'

Bendix looked at her. 'The only thing that puzzles me,' he said, 'is why you've started up again. I heard about the stage robbery. There's talk of a train being held up. The outlaws blew the safe. It's not difficult to put one and one together.'

She stared back at him and there was anger now burning in her eyes.

'Yes, the Presidio Kid did those things,' she said. She leaned towards him. 'Maybe things would have been different if it hadn't been for this.' She pointed at her cheek across which the scar was flaming, 'I got branded just like cattle, just like I was a cow critter. It was dynamite that did it; it was gettin' careless that caused me to lose everything.'

'Then why put everything at risk again? You put your takings to good use. You've got the biggest spread in the territory. Why start it all again now?'

'Why?' she shouted. 'You ask me why? Because since Gilpin left me I've been slowly dyin'. Do you think I really care a hoot for any of this? I tried, how I tried, but it's been like bein' buried alive. When that low-down bounty hunter found out about Gilpin's whereabouts it was like comin' alive again. I guess it was foolish, but I really began to hope. I began to hope that things might be like they used to be. Maybe Gilpin would come back to me. Maybe we could pick it up again. Maybe . . . but I figured: why wait? Why pin everythin' on Gilpin comin' back to me? Besides, if he did he would want the same thing as me. He wouldn't want a life with no thrills, no adventure. He would want to take his place just like before. So I got the gang together and we started to ride again. The Presidio Kid is back and still no-one knows her true identity.'

She turned to Bendix. 'Except you

184

now,' she said. 'Except you.'

There was no mistaking the menace in her tones, but her conversation took an unexpected turn.

'You were a friend of Gilpin,' she mused. 'You looked after him at the end.' She got to her feet, seized the whiskey bottle and poured from it.

'What sort of a life do you lead?' she said. 'Are you satisfied with it?'

Bendix did not reply. He was suddenly thinking of Miranda Coolidge.

'Why don't you join us?' she said, then paused, as if considering the idea for the first time. 'Yes,' she continued, 'why not join us? You know how to take care of yourself. I've heard how you dealt with that idiot Barrett. Don't you see? You don't have to be a range bum. You don't have to punch cows. Whatever it is you do now, you could be somebody. What do you say? Do you really want to go on as you are? This could be your chance.'

Bendix was thinking fast. There was something slightly deranged about this woman who called herself the Presidio Kid. She had him in her power and he didn't rate his chances of survival very high if he tried to escape from the Rocking-Horse. At the same time, the Presidio Kid was dangerous. Apart from the fact that she was threatening the other ranchers and aiming to take over their spreads, she had resumed her outlaw activities, robbing and killing. The Presidio Kid and her gang needed to be stopped. If there was any chance of doing it and of staying alive in the process, what other way was there than to accept her offer? There would be danger enough, but if he could be accepted, even if only temporarily, as a member of the gang, then maybe he could find out what was the next target and have a chance of spiking her plans. Maybe he could get word to the marshal or to Coolidge. Basically, there was no other option.

'You mean it?' he said. 'You ain't puttin' me on?'

'Puttin' you on? Of course not. I'm

givin' you an option. You won't get another like it.'

She turned to him, her features now eager and excited. 'You were Gilpin's friend. That's why I'm saying this, that's why I'm making you this offer. Ride with the Presidio Kid and you'll never look back. Take your chance now you have it. Can't you understand what I'm saying?'

Bendix smiled. 'Hell yes,' he said. 'You're right. This is my chance unless I want to stay a no-worth cow-puncher for the rest of my days.'

Miss Otilie raised her glass. 'OK.' She laughed. 'Let's drink to it. Here's to the two of us. From now on you ride with the Presidio Kid.'

He lifted his glass and they drank.

'I'll get the boys to ride over to the ranch with you,' she said. 'I've got some business to finish here. Put your horse up at the stable and make yourself at home in the bunkhouse. We'll talk again tomorrow.'

When he had gone she lay back

against the cushions before pouring herself another drink. She could hear the sound of hoofs in the yard outside. Suddenly she felt a surge of loneliness; she intended to finish that bottle.

★ ★ ★

Marshal Mercer stepped back from the window of his office.

'Wonder what Bendix wants with that Craven *hombre* from the Rocking-Horse?'

'You mean Miss Otilie's foreman?' his deputy replied.

'Yeah. The pair of 'em just rode out of town. I never liked the look of that man. Never trusted him.'

The marshal paced the room for a while then strode to the door. 'You take care of things here,' he said. 'I'm takin' a ride to the Tumbling W. See how Luke Grey is gettin' along. After that I might drop in on Seb Coolidge at the Eleven Half-Circle.'

He went out through the door and

stepped into the saddle of his horse which was tethered to the rail outside. As he rode off he was thinking about what he had just seen. He was hearing stories of a train robbery outside of Cedar Slide. That was outside his jurisdiction but it troubled him. Taken together with the stage holdup it pointed to a resurgence of trouble that seemed to have died out a long whiles before. He had enough troubles with Miss Otilie and the Rocking-Horse.

When he got to the Tumbling W he was relieved to find Luke Grey in much better condition. He was sitting up and his whole attitude seemed to have taken a turn for the better.

'Marshal,' he said as Mercer entered the room. 'Good to see you.'

'Thought I'd stop by, see how you are.'

'Well, you can see for yourself. I'm a lot better.'

The marshal sat by the bed and held his hat in his hands. 'Hope you don't mind,' he said, 'but I dropped by Drake

Jordan's office. I managed to persuade him not to finalize any sales but I can't stall him much longer.'

'There ain't goin' to be no sales,' Grey said. 'I've changed my mind about the whole thing.'

The marshal jumped up. 'You don't mean it?' he said.

'By Jiminy, I do mean it. Those bushwhackin' buzzards nearly done for me but I'm almost fit again. There's no way I'm gonna let them beat me. I don't know how they persuaded me to sign those papers, but whatever it was it was done under duress.'

The marshal seized him by the arm. 'I'm right glad to hear it,' he said. 'I knowed there was somethin' fishy about the whole thing. It's not like you to give way to pressure.'

The rancher grinned sheepishly. 'I feel bad about it,' he said. 'I'm just kinda worried now in case things have gone too far. However it happened, I signed some papers. Does that mean I've no longer any rights to the

Tumbling W? That lawyer had me tied up in knots. What if I've signed the ranch away?'

'Leave that to me,' Mercer replied. 'Just carry on getting better.' He stood up and put his hat on his head.

'I'll be back,' he said.

He mounted his horse and rode off in the direction of the Eleven Half-Circle, where he was greeted by Seb Coolidge.

'I thought Bendix was stayin' with you?' he said.

Coolidge held a finger to his lips. 'Don't want Miranda hearing anything,' he said. 'Truth is Coolidge left this mornin'. He's puttin' up at the hotel.'

In a few words he told the marshal about Bendix's plan to flush out the Rocking-Horse connection with the events which had taken place. When he had finished the marshal looked thoughtful.

'That explains why I saw Bendix riding out with Craven earlier.'

'Miss Otilie's foreman?'

The marshal nodded. 'He could be

lettin' himself in for a heap of trouble,' he said.

'I reckon Bendix can take care of himself.'

'Yeah, I expect he can,' the marshal replied.

The marshal took his leave and rode slowly back to Horse Bend. He was still rather confused about what was happening, but he sensed that things were drawing to a head. Whatever was going on, it spelled trouble.

*   *   *

There was a game of cards going on in the bunkhouse that evening as Bendix entered and was shown to a bunk. A couple of the players looked up but made no comment. On the ride over from the line cabin Craven had been surly but otherwise had shown no overt antagonism. Bendix guessed that Miss Otilie had had a word with him. He lay back and, trying to ignore the noise and chatter, started to go over his encounter with Miss Otilie.

Although he had suspected it and now knew it was true, he still could not quite believe that she was the Presidio Kid. She had done a pretty good job of concealing it. He wondered whether anybody else knew, and if so, how many. He thought about his old friend Gilpin. He had found it hard to believe that he had been involved with any outlaw activity when Marshal Jennings had shown him the Wanted poster, but it was all true. He recollected the times they had ridden together, searching for any clue to Gilpin's subsequent behaviour, but he could find none.

Giving up on that line of thought, he wondered instead about how things were back in Driftwood. He had no concerns about Jennings's ability to sort out any trouble that the Rocking-Horse men might have been causing, but something was worrying at his mind. He turned things over and over and then he had it. Driftwood was a long ways off. Why were they still hanging about there? Miss Otilie — he still thought of her in those terms — had told him she had dispatched some of her ranch hands to look for Gilpin. Was there something else involved, something she hadn't told him?

The more he thought about it the more likely it seemed. He could understand her not going herself; if Gilpin was to be found and if they were to have any chance of a life together, she would want to meet him on her own ground. But some of those Rocking-Horse riders had been gone a long time. They had taken a lot of pains to locate the cabin. Was the break which had taken place between Gilpin and the Presidio Kid just a lover's quarrel?

Gilpin had built his cabin in a lonely, inaccessible place. Was that solely because he wanted to nurse his emotional wounds in secret? What other reason could there be? Come to that, had Bolton Moss sought out Gilpin's hiding-place only because of the bounty? If there was more to it than he had been led to believe, then the additional factor must involve money.

He started to think about the cabin, to go over it in his mind. He had not lived there for very long, but the place was small and he had got to know it pretty well. There was no place there that money could have been concealed without him finding it.

The sound of laughter suddenly awakened him from his reverie to the present moment. The card game had broken up and the players were seeking their own bunks. It was late and they were ready to call it a day. Someone turned down a lamp and Bendix turned his face to the wall, seeking sleep. He was likely to need all his wits about him tomorrow and on the succeeding days.

His thought turned to Miranda. She wouldn't be pleased to find him gone. Still, he had acted for the best and there was no point in worrying about that now, but he couldn't help thinking about the way she had looked and felt when he held her close. That had been only the previous evening but it seemed like a long time ago. Events had moved fast since, but then that was true of their whole relationship. Maybe that was the way it was when a man lived from day to day, not knowing when his time might come. Suddenly his time had become precious.

The following day Bendix was assigned the task of combing the breaks for some cattle under the close supervision of the same two riders who had followed him and Craven from Horse Bend. Once or twice, thinking he might be able to garner some information about the cattle rustling, he attempted to make conversation but they were giving nothing away. It seemed to Bendix that, while the pair of them might be sufficiently skilled to be able to round up a few old mossyhorns, they were not natural cowpunchers. All the time they were working they continued to wear both guns tied down with a thong.

At noon they ate some jerky and

biscuit and made coffee before going back into the brush but they weren't very successful. Occasionally they would find small groups of cattle but most of the draws were empty. It was hard work too, at least for Bendix, and as the afternoon wore on he began to wonder why Miss Otilie would bother with the few strays they were picking up. She was in charge of a huge operation, so what difference would a few old critters make?

He came to the conclusion that she was just keeping him occupied, giving him something to do away from the ranch. In which case, if there was nothing better to occupy him, did it mean that it was time already for the next raid to take place? What would it be? Another stage? Another railroad train?

Towards the middle of the afternoon they had gathered no more than a couple of dozen cattle and they began to haze them back towards the ranch. When they got back and had penned the cattle in one of the corrals, Miss

Otilie herself appeared.

'Bendix,' she called, 'when you've cleaned up, come over to the ranch house. I want to have a word with you.'

When he entered she poured him a cup of coffee. She was wearing a white blouse with a long skirt. With her trim figure and short hair she looked quite prim and Bendix found himself questioning whether she could truly be the infamous Presidio Kid. When he had settled in a chair her first words were enough to dispel any doubts.

'Mr Bendix, how have you enjoyed your first day riding for the Rocking-Horse?'

Bendix shrugged, 'I've enjoyed better company,' he said.

She gave a short laugh. 'Well, be thankful that it's only for one day.' She looked across at him. 'Do you still feel the same way you did last night? About takin' your opportunity, about not endin' up like those two no-hopers?'

'You mean about ridin' with . . . ' He paused, not sure whether to say 'the

Presidio Kid' or simply 'you'.

'The Presidio Kid,' she answered for him.

'Yes, the Presidio Kid. Sounds good, don't it?' he replied. 'Like I said, I ain't gonna get another chance. I'm tired of bein' a nobody, a range bum. Believe me, I'm ready to take this chance with both hands.'

She laughed again. 'Now don't go layin' it on too thick,' she said. 'You realize that once you cross the line there ain't no going back? You'll be outside the law. You'll be a wanted man.'

'Sure, but what have I got to lose?'

'I don't know. What have you got to lose?'

He glanced at her. She was looking at him with a strange expression on her face. The side with the scar was turned away and she looked in that instant quite beautiful and almost girlish.

'I'm here, aren't I?' he said.

'You didn't have much choice.' She dropped her eyes. 'Enough of this,' she said. 'I'm glad you feel the way you do.

You won't regret it. And to show that I believe you, I can tell you that we ride the day after tomorrow.'

'Yeah! That's great. I didn't want to be kickin' my heels brush-poppin' or mendin' fences or whatever else you might have had in line for me.'

She laughed again. 'Oh, Mr Bendix, trust me. I have other things in line for you than either of those.'

'So what is it? What are we gonna hit?'

She looked up at him again, regarding him closely. 'Do you need to know?' she asked.

Bendix realized he needed to be careful. Maybe she had meant more than she said when she had commented about him laying it on thick. He must be careful not to overplay his hand. Before he could say anything, however, she resumed the conversation herself.

'No, I don't mind tellin' you,' she said. 'You see, I trust you. You were Ed Gilpin's friend. He trusted you and so do I.'

For a moment they continued looking at each other.

'The Pecos and South-Western Bank,' she said.

Bendix was caught by surprise. He had expected another attack on a stage or a train, but nothing as brash as this. So far as he was aware, the Presidio Kid had not attempted anything like that before. Hitting the bank was a different proposition. In terms of the element of danger involved, maybe it was no more risky than the other jobs, but it seemed to carry the business to a new level of audacity. She was bringing her style of lawlessness right to the centre of the community, right to the beating heart of Horse Bend. There was a big chance of someone being recognized but she didn't seem to care. It was as though she was deliberately throwing down a challenge as her confidence grew.

'The bank,' he replied. 'Well, I guess that's the best place to find the money.'

'Yes. And there'll be plenty of it. I happen to know that some big deposits have been made recently. The town is expanding. There are businessmen with an eye to the main chance. Despite them both suffering some recent losses, the stage company has been doing well and there's talk of linking the town to the railroad. The bank is like a turkey just waitin' to be plucked.'

Jordan, Bendix thought, *Drake Jordan*. Where else would she get her information?

'And to show how much I trust you,' she resumed, 'I'm givin' you a key role.'

'Yeah? What's that?'

'You'll be the one to go into the bank and start the whole shebang. Whoever's in there, you get them to be quiet while you deal with the teller.'

'Deal with the teller?'

'You don't have to shoot him. Just make sure you get the keys to the safe and get into the manager's office before he even realizes what's going on. Craven will be right behind you.'

Bendix thought for a moment. 'Wouldn't it be simpler if you just went in and asked to see the manager? You're a big-shot customer.'

'I'd thought of that. Sounds reasonable, but everyone would know me without my disguise. Besides, I ain't much good at actin' and I like to keep away from town.'

Bendix had a sudden intuition. 'And you like people to know that it's the Presidio Kid who's involved.'

For a second her blue eyes flashed. 'Yes, you're right, Mr Bendix. I want everyone to know when the Presidio Kid strikes. I want people to know just exactly who is pullin' the strings. I guess a part of me always wanted to be famous.'

'This ain't like takin' a stagecoach,' Bendix said. 'I don't see how you can be involved without people either knowin' who you are or bein' put on their guard by that mask you wear.'

'Which brings us back to why you are going to enter the building and not me.'

'But you'll be there.'

'I'll be there,' she replied.

Bendix finished the last of his coffee. 'Well, whatever you aim to do, I'm just glad to be part of it,' he said.

Miss Otilie got to her feet. 'I think this calls for something stronger than coffee,' she said. 'Let's drink to taking the Pecos and South-Western Bank. Let's drink to all the other capers we'll be pullin' while I fill you in with the details.'

7

Things were quiet in the town of Horse Bend. A few people passed along the boardwalks, going to and from the various stores. In his workshop Joe Thompson, the blacksmith, leaned against a post and wiped his hand across his brow. It was hot inside the forge and a cloud of steam rose into the air as he dipped hot metal into a bucket of water. One or two customers had gathered in the café where the waitress was pouring coffee. A buckboard travelled down the street, pursued by a barking dog.

On the veranda outside the saloon old Billy Warren lounged as usual in his rocking-chair and spat from time to time in the dust of the road. Some horses were tied at the hitch racks. A few miles outside of town little Jimmy Thurston was fishing in a deep pool in a bend of the river when he heard the sound of horses' hoofs. He looked up and saw a group of riders in the distance. He watched as they came closer, riding at a leisurely rate, then lost sight of them as they turned a bend and disappeared down another trail. Their dust hung in the air.

While they were still some distance from town, the Presidio Kid held up her hand and the riders came to a halt in a grove of cottonwoods. Some of them already had their bandannas pulled up. The Presidio Kid was wearing one of the long black 'yashmaks' which covered her whole face from the brows to below the chin. The eyeholes were mere slits and when she spoke the silk fabric gently expanded and contracted. Her hair was concealed beneath a black hat and she had taken pains to disguise her identity so that no-one would have suspected that she was a woman. Again Bendix wondered how many people were in on her secret.

'Right,' she said. 'Everyone knows

what they're doing?'

Some of the riders answered in muted monosyllables, some of them merely nodded.

'Jackson and Lonsdale will wait outside with the horses. Bendix and Craven will enter the bank. Two of you wait here just in case any extra support is needed when we ride back along the trail. Williams and Jaeger will be under cover ready to deal with the marshal if he puts in an appearance. I will be with the rest of the boys ready to come in shootin'. Once we get past this spot we split up and after that each man makes his own way back to the Rocking-Horse. Just make sure nobody ain't tailin' you.'

Bendix looked at Craven. Craven's eyes were flat and empty.

'Let's ride!'

At the Presidio Kid's words they dug in their spurs and started down the trail. Part of the way along they divided, aiming to enter town at different points. Bendix and Craven, together with the two who had been assigned the job of waiting with the horses, rode together. Bendix had spent a good part of the night fretting over how he might get word to the marshal but he could think of nothing. There was no way of doing it. He would just have to play things by ear.

They had only a short ride before they hit town. After entering the main street by way of side alleys, they tied their horses to a hitch rack on the opposite side of the street to the bank. Bendix and Craven dismounted. Bendix looked up and down the street but it was quiet and he could see no sign of Mercer. He felt curiously exposed as he and Craven crossed the street, then mounted the sidewalk outside the bank. He was struck again by the Presidio Kid's egotism in choosing the bank for her target. Not many people knew him but there must be a good chance of someone recognizing any of the riders from the Rocking-Horse. Maybe she had chosen people who rarely came to town, like herself. All the same, she seemed to be putting her neck out. Wouldn't it have been simpler to have attacked another stagecoach?

He had no time to pursue these thoughts. They were standing outside the doors of the bank. Bendix glanced at Craven, who nodded at him and put his hand towards his neckerchief. He opened the door and Bendix preceded him into the bank.

It was very quiet. Only one person stood at the counter. The clerk looked up as they entered, then reached behind the desk. The door to the manager's office stood partly open. Bendix's eyes quickly swept the room. There was nothing unusual but he sensed something was wrong. The place was too quiet. There was no conversation between the customer at the counter and the bank clerk, whose hands were still behind the counter. The only sound was the buzzing of a fly. There was nothing to be done for the moment but carry out instructions. Drawing his gun, he stepped forward.

'OK,' he rapped. 'Don't anybody do anythin' stupid!'

The teller looked up again. For the fraction of a second their eyes met and Bendix could see that there was something other than fear in the man's eyes. At the same instant the man at the counter spun aside to reveal the muzzle of a sawn-down shotgun in the teller's hands. Out of the corner of his eye Bendix saw Craven with a gun in his hand but it wasn't pointed towards the bank clerk. It was pointed at him. There was a gun in the hands of the customer who had stepped away from the counter.

In an instant Bendix knew that he was betrayed. He spun round and fired at Craven at almost the same moment that Craven's gun spat lead at him. Craven was a fraction too slow and Bendix's bullet caught him full in the chest, sending him crashing backwards as his own gun exploded into the air.

The bullet ricocheted and fragments of plaster fell from the ceiling, causing just enough of a distraction for the bank teller's blast of buckshot to go mostly wide of the mark. Bendix felt a sting of pain in his shoulder as he leaped to one side and began to zigzag for the entrance. The door to the manager's office flew open behind him and someone emerged.

'Stop right there, Bendix!' a voice boomed.

Without looking back, Bendix recognized it as the marshal's. Another shot rang out but Bendix had already crashed through the door. Hesitating for only a moment, he saw the Rocking-Horse riders across the street draw their guns. Bent low, he fired under his arm and one of them dropped from his horse. Then he was round the corner of the bank and running pell-mell down an alley which ran the length of the bank.

Shots rang out behind him and went whistling nearby as he rounded the corner and began to sprint along a backstreet. A man walking along in the opposite direction gave him a strange look, then, as another shot went whining overhead, dived to the floor, crawling to the shelter of a doorway.

Bendix turned and entered another passageway which led to yet another, then he emerged back on the main street near a saloon. Outside a couple of horses were tethered. Quickly he untied one of them, a rangy looking skewbald. He leaped into the saddle, turned and galloped off in the opposite direction to the bank.

A few people passing in the street stood and watched as he hurtled by. There were shouts coming from behind him and a couple of shots rang out but there was no attempt to stop him and soon he was beyond the last buildings and speeding away into the country. As he rode he became aware again of the pain in his shoulder. He had been hit by a .00 buckshot ball; it was bleeding but it wasn't serious.

He knew now why he had felt so exposed when he and Craven moved towards the bank. He had been set up. The whole bank job had been an elaborate charade to get him killed. The Presidio Kid must have tipped off the marshal. But why would she do it? Wouldn't it have been a lot simpler just to have had him killed while he was at the Rocking-Horse?

There were two reasons that he could think of. By framing him, she might distract the law from ever looking in her direction for those stage and railroad robberies. They would probably be put down to him. But more than that, it seemed to fit in with what he had come to learn of her character. She craved drama and excitement; she relished the grandiose gesture. That was why, despite her denials, she took such pride in her possessions, why she had put up that unnecessary sign at the outskirts of her domain. To kill him quietly would have been too easy, too boring. She had to do things in a more elaborate fashion. She couldn't resist the opportunity to make a theatrical production of it.

But why had she taken an objection to him? He had read her wrong there. She wasn't sympathetic to him because of his friendship with Gilpin. Quite the opposite. She must have resented it and, made bitter by her disappointment in not meeting Gilpin again, she had reacted in the way she had. Now he had more of an understanding of how she and Gilpin might have parted. She was a dangerous lady to be associated with.

His thoughts were interrupted when he saw two riders coming towards him whom he recognized as the ones who had been left behind when the rest of the gang rode into town. He veered away from the trail, and rode hard across some broken country. Looking back, he could see them following him, but they were a long way behind. He crested a rise and slowed the horse to a trot, seeking cover. He spotted a grove of cottonwood trees and rode the skewbald into them.

He waited, his gun in his hand, till the two riders appeared. They were checking the ground for sign and coming on slowly. Then they stopped and one of them said something to the other. They looked across towards the trees where Bendix sat his horse and one of them drew his rifle from its scabbard. Bendix waited, calculating how close he would allow them to come before he opened fire.

For a few minutes the riders continued to sit their horses, then one of them spoke to the other once more. They both looked across at the trees and continued to talk together. Then they turned their horses and started to ride away in the direction from which they had come.

Bendix waited till he felt sure they were well out of sight, then rode back out of the cover of the trees. He guessed that the riders, unwilling to take any chances, had decided to ride back and rejoin their companions. After that there was no doubt in Bendix's mind that they would be coming after him. And it wouldn't only be the Presidio Kid he had to deal with. The marshal would be pursuing him as well. Right now he was probably rounding up a posse. The question facing Bendix was what he intended doing about it.

His first thought was to ride for the Eleven Half-Circle. He could be certain of getting a welcome there, but then he didn't want to put Miranda into any danger. He could return to town and try to persuade the marshal of his innocence, but that would be a very risky thing to do.

Then he was struck by a thought. The marshal had been tipped off about him, but he had no proof that Bendix was involved. Sure, he had called out his name, but Bendix had been masked. The marshal was reacting to what he had been told.

Then another thought occurred to him. The first person he had fired at, the only person he had shot, was

Craven, and the marshal's doubts about that individual were on the record. Maybe the marshal could be persuaded after all? It was worth a try. Trouble was, the Presidio Kid, or some of her gang, might still be waiting in town. Thinking it over further, he decided it was a risk he had to take. He pulled at the reins and turned his mount back towards Horse Bend.

He hadn't ridden very far when he saw a cloud of dust moving towards him. It could be either the posse or the Presidio Kid with her gang. He pulled up and watched to see in which direction it was headed. It was going north and east, in the direction of the Rocking-Horse. Bendix watched for a while till the cloud vanished. There was no way of knowing, but he was willing to bet that the Presidio Kid was heading back to her ranch. He expected the gang to come looking for him. He had no doubt that they would, but maybe they had other business to attend to. He dug his spurs into the horse's side and made for town.

When he arrived there was a lot of activity. A crowd of people still hung about the bank and a wagon was drawn up outside the doctor's house. Nobody seemed to take much notice of Bendix. He tied his horse to a hitch rack and made for the marshal's office. Down that end of town, away from the bank, it was much quieter. Bendix was uncertain what to expect. Would the marshal be there, or would he already be out looking for him? Suddenly the silence was shattered as a shot rang out, whistling by Bendix's ear. It came from a side alley and Bendix dropped to one knee, drawing and firing in one smooth motion. Another shot rang out, tearing up the ground near his feet, but this one came from a different direction. Bendix rolled to the partial cover of the overhang of the sidewalk. As he did so a voice called:

'Bendix! To your left!'

Bendix looked up to see a figure emerging from a side passage with a rifle in his hands. He recognized the man as one of the Presidio Kid's gang. The man had him covered but Bendix's gun spoke first and the man reeled back. He still held the rifle, however, and as he raised it another shot rang out. This time he threw up the weapon and fell backwards to the ground, where he lay unmoving. From the other alleyway there came the sound of running feet. In an instant Bendix was up and plunging after him. As he entered the passage another shot whistled over his head, then the man disappeared around a corner. Bendix continued running. As he emerged into the open he could see the man running hard away from him. Bendix had just raised his gun when another figure stepped out into the path ahead of the running man. Bendix recognized the marshal.

'Stop right there!'

The man drew to a sudden halt. For a few moments he seemed to hesitate.

'Drop your gun now or you're dead!'

The man glanced slightly behind him to see the figure of Bendix at his rear. Seeing that the game was up, he threw his weapon away and held up his hands as the marshal and Bendix advanced on him.

'Didn't expect to see you back in town,' the marshal said.

'Am I under arrest as well as this *hombre?*'

'Guess I ought to put you behind bars, but we'll see. You sure got some explainin' to do.'

Motioning with his gun, the marshal started in the direction of the jailhouse. When they got there he put the man in the same cell as his other prisoner from the Rocking-Horse, then he returned to his office. Bendix had dropped on to a chair. His shoulder was hurting and all the exercise had caused the wound to start bleeding afresh.

'Guess you better see the doc,' Mercer said.

Bendix waved his hand. 'Maybe later. First of all I'd better start explainin'' what this is all about.'

The marshal poured a couple of shots of bourbon. 'Drink that,' he said.

Bendix held his head back and tossed it down his throat. It felt good as it burned its way down.

'I know what this is all about,' the marshal said. 'Most of it, anyways. You can fill me in with the details.'

Bendix looked surprised.

'Drake Jordan has been talkin'. I've had him in my sights for a while. He told me how some of the Rocking-Horse boys were runnin' out of control and how they planned to set you up. I think they figured to get some loot for themselves in the process. Don't know how they expected to get away with it. Maybe it would have worked but, like I say, Jordan got cold feet. He's told me all about the pressure Miss Otilie has been applyin' to get hold of the Tumbling W and the Eleven Half-Circle. I'm gonna have to ride out there and put her under arrest. There's a little matter of cattle-rustlin' to take into account as well.'

Bendix looked closely at him. 'There's more than that,' he said.

'Yeah? What's that then?'

'I guess Jordan didn't know. You maybe won't believe this, Marshal, but Miss Otilie is none other than the Presidio Kid.'

The marshal's jaw dropped. He poured another glass of bourbon and swallowed it in one mouthful. Then he whistled.

'I can prove it,' Bendix said. 'She organized the bank caper and she was also behind the railroad attack and the stage hold-up.'

The marshal rubbed his hands across his hair. 'You know, come to think of it, it would make some sense. But you better carry on with your explanation.'

Before Bendix could begin the door to the marshal's office opened and the doctor came in.

'Two men lyin' dead out in the street,' he said. 'Someone said I might be needed here.'

The marshal pointed towards Bendix. 'He was just about to tell me somethin',' he said. 'You can listen if you like. I think you'll find it very interestin'.'

* * *

It was early in the morning and the sun's rays were just lightening the horizon as a group of riders approached the Rocking-Horse. They had come over from the Eleven Half-Circle, where Bendix had spent the night before being joined by the marshal, Coolidge and Luke Grey, now more or less fully recovered from the beating he had received, together with a number of other citizens of Horse Bend. Mercer had thought it best not to let the news about the identity of Miss Otilie become widely known. There was no knowing what effect it might have. He was not expecting trouble but he was prepared. What he wasn't prepared for was the strange sense of emptiness he felt as they crossed Rocking-Horse territory, and it wasn't just that it was early in the day.

'Somethin' odd around here,' he said to Bendix.

'Know what you mean. Don't know what it is, but somethin' don't feel right.' As they approached the ranch house in the fresh light of day there was no sign of activity. No smoke ascended from the chimneys of the hacienda or the bunkhouse. Cattle were gathered in the corrals but there were few horses. They clattered into the yard but they remained in their saddles and looked about them while the marshal dropped to the ground and stepped up to the door. He rapped loudly but there was no reply. He rapped again, then turned as the door to one of the barns opened and a man approached.

'Howdy,' the man said. 'I bin half expectin' you.'

'We've come to speak with Miss Otilie,' the marshal replied.

'Miss Otilie ain't here.'

'What do you mean, she isn't here?'

'Like I say, she's gone. Rode out yesterday with a whole bunch of her riders.'

The marshal looked towards the others.

'Where did she go?' Coolidge shouted.

The man shrugged his shoulders. 'Miss Otilie doesn't tell me her plans. All I know is that she rode off with a gang of the others yesterday mornin' and said she might be gone a whiles.'

'So who's lookin' after the ranch?' the marshal said.

'There's enough of us remainin'. Ain't like she's not left the place before.'

The marshal climbed back into leather. 'If Miss Otilie comes back,' he said, 'tell her to come and see me.'

The man touched his hand to his forehead as they rode out of the yard. They continued riding for a while before drawing to a halt.

'What now?' the marshal said.

'Guess there's nothin' we can do,' Luke Grey replied. 'It's a damned pity.

I can't wait to get my hands on those dry-gulchin' varmints that pistol-whipped me.'

'You might still get your chance,' the marshal said.

All the way back to Horse Bend Bendix was thinking about things. This time the Presidio Kid had gone too far. In a fit of hubris she had acted rashly and blown her cover. South-west Texas had become too hot for her. At least for the time being she needed new territory. The man they had spoken to had said that Miss Otilie had told him she might be gone for a while. Suddenly he knew where she was going with the rest of her gang. She was heading for Wyoming. She was riding for Driftwood and then for the mountains where her lover had sought shelter. All the while Bendix had had a feeling that the denouement of the whole affair would take place where he had first been drawn into it, at Gilpin's cabin.

Bendix was still unsure whether there might have been something else behind the split which had taken place between the Presidio Kid and Gilpin. Perhaps Gilpin had built his retreat not just because of the break-up of his relationship with the Presidio Kid but because he was hiding from the rest of the gang. Had he double-crossed them? Although there were aspects of Gilpin's character which had escaped Bendix, he felt he had known him well enough to know that he wouldn't do that. Besides, there was no record of the gang being broken up or any mass arrest of the outlaws. Above all, the Presidio Kid's identity had remained a secret — until now. Gilpin had not given her away. So was money behind the rift?

When they had reached town and the rest of the party had gone their separate ways, Bendix approached the marshal with his reflections. The marshal didn't need a lot of persuading that Bendix was probably right.

'Question is, what we do about it?' he commented. 'I could get up a posse but my jurisdiction doesn't extend that far.'

'You're needed here,' Bendix replied. 'So are the others. It's a long ways to Driftwood for a party of riders but not so far for someone riding alone. We need to act quick. Time is now the major factor.'

'What are you sayin'?'

'I'll ride to Driftwood. With any luck I might get there at about the same time as the Kid.'

'What could you do alone against a whole parcel of the coyotes?'

'I wouldn't be alone. You're forgettin' Jennings. There were two of us rode down to Texas. There'll be two of us back in Wyoming.'

The marshal rose to his feet and paced a few times up and down the floor.

'Can't say as I like it,' he said, 'but I can see your point.'

'I'm ready to go right now,' Bendix said.

'What about that shoulder?'

'It's fine. Nothin' more than a scratch.' He hesitated. 'Just one thing bothers me,' he said. 'I feel bad about

Miss Miranda. She looked after me real good when I was hurt and . . . well, we've grown kinda close.'

There was a smile on the marshal's face. 'Don't worry,' he said. 'Leave Miss Miranda to me. I'll explain to her how it is. She might take some pacifyin' but I think she might just relent.'

A slow embarrassed grin spread across Bendix's features. He held out his hand. 'Sure appreciate it,' he said.

'I'll send a message up the line,' the marshal said. 'Let Jennings know you're on your way.'

⋆　⋆　⋆

Bendix rode hard, hoping to come up with the Presidio Kid and her gang, but they seemed to be pushing on quickly too. Bendix guessed that she was keen to reach the cabin. A couple of times he saw a dust cloud in the distance which might or might not have been them. He wasn't sure what he would find when he reached Driftwood. When at last he

229

rode into town it was to find things looking peaceful and normal. He smiled to himself as he swung down from the saddle and walked into Jennings's office.

'Why, you old son of a gun,' Jennings said, jumping to his feet, 'it's good to see you again.'

'Good to be back,' Bendix replied.

'The telegraph man passed on the message you were headed this way but there wasn't much about the reason why,' Jennings said. A knowing grin spread across his face. 'I would have guessed you had more reason to stay in Horse Bend,' he added.

Ignoring this last remark, Bendix set about explaining how things were. When he had finished the marshal drew his familiar bottle of whiskey from the top drawer of his desk and poured them both a drink.

'Well,' he said, 'I can't hardly believe it. Miss Otilie Stevens — the Presidio Kid! And you say she's headed this way?'

'You ain't seen nothin' of her around town?'

'Nope. And I ain't seen nothin' of those Rocking-Horse varmints since I ran 'em out of town neither.'

'You have much trouble with 'em?' Bendix asked.

'Nothin' I couldn't handle. Guess I made a mistake leavin' a tenderfoot in charge in the first place.'

Bendix was pondering the situation. 'If the Presidio Kid ain't turned up in Driftwood,' he said, 'my guess is that she's headed straight for the mountains. Reckon I need to get out there pretty darn quick.'

'Correction,' the marshal said. 'We need to get out there pretty damn quick.'

Bendix looked up over his glass. 'Might mean leavin' the tenderfoot in charge again,' he said.

'Morris has learned some now. Guess he's well on his way to becomin' a regular town-tamer.'

They finished their drinks and

Jennings poured another. 'Give me an hour to arrange things here,' he said, 'and then we'll ride.'

★　★　★

Coming up the trail from the foothills, there was plenty of sign to tell Bendix and Jennings that a considerable number of riders had passed that way, and recently.

'Do any of 'em know the way to the cabin?' the marshal said.

'Reckon so,' Bendix replied.

They rode on till the trail began to grow steep. The ears of the steeldust were pricked and Jennings's horse was skittish. When they rounded a corner they found the reason why. Lying amongst the scrub were a dead horse and rider. It was clear that they must have fallen. Bendix looked up the trail ahead of them to where it could only be negotiated single file.

'Must have taken them a good whiles to get up beyond that,' Bendix said. 'They can't be far ahead of us.'

Jennings pondered the situation. 'No point in lettin' them know we're comin',' he said. 'Might be an idea if we dismount and leave the horses here.'

'Just what I was thinkin'. And I got another idea. Assumin' they've found the cabin, instead of comin' at 'em head on, why don't we take a little detour and drop down from behind? Take 'em by surprise.'

'It'll be the only advantage we have,' Jennings replied.

'I lived here for a time, remember. There's a path leads above the cabin and brings you out in the trees behind.'

'What are we waitin' for?'

They picketed the horses and moved forward on foot. Even without their mounts it was a hairy route to follow. The trail clung to the side of the cliff and fell abruptly away on the other side to a sheer drop of hundreds of feet. Looking over the edge caused Jennings to feel giddy. Bendix had ridden down the trail before but even he felt uneasy. Taking it slowly, they climbed higher till the trail began to widen out. A little further and they were approaching the spot where Bolton Moss had lain in wait for Bendix before firing the shot which had shattered his knee. Off to the right was a slight cleft in the rock wall.

'Here,' Bendix said. 'It looks like nothin' but there's a way out.'

They slipped into the gap and they moved forward for a few steps till they were confronted by some rocks and boulders. Bendix, leading the way, began to climb over them till he dropped down into a narrow, dry streambed that led steeply upwards. They scrambled on, at times on their hands and knees, until they came at last to a spot where the banks were less sheer. Taking hold of whatever vegetation offered a handhold, Bendix heaved himself up till he came out on the slope of the mountain, sheltered by bushes and concealed from the cabin by the overhanging cliff face. Jennings, panting for breath, clambered up behind him.

'Listen,' Bendix whispered.

The wind was coming over the mountain ridge towards the cabin, but they could still distinctly hear the sound of voices and the snickering of horses.

'Follow me, but be careful not to make any sound,' Bendix said.

They pushed their way through the bushes and then, bent almost double, moved forward till they were close to the cliff edge when they dropped to the ground and slithered forward the rest of the way. Taking great care, they peered down at the scene below.

They were behind the cabin which cut off part of their view of what was happening, but they could see a number of men milling about in front. Some were on horseback. Presently the others began to move towards their horses and then a figure emerged into their field of vision, a figure in black and wearing a strange black mask.

'The Presidio Kid!' Bendix whispered. He was straining his ears to catch something of what was being said but the wind carried the sound away.

Broken fragments reached him:

'Nothin'.'

'Somewhere else.'

'Ready to blow.'

Bendix, recalling something of the Presidio Kid's methods, seized Jennings by the arm.

'Dynamite!' he breathed. 'They're goin' to blow up the cabin.'

'Hell,' Jennings said. 'I hope they've got the charge right. This whole cliff face could come down.'

Bendix had a sinking feeling in his stomach. The Presidio Kid had been reckless about her identity. She had almost gone out of her way to make it known. He had put it down to hubris. Now he realized with a sickening feeling that there was an extra element. The Presidio Kid was out of control. Whether it was because of the disappointment and anguish of not finding Gilpin, whether it was because of her doomed love for Bendix's former friend, she was now engaged in a desperate final act of self-destruction and she didn't care whom she took with her.

'Start movin'!' he rapped.

The two of them slithered back. Then they got to their feet and began to run. At the same moment there came a shattering explosion and a crump of air which flung them off their feet and threw them to the ground as if they were rag dolls. Bendix felt the ground shake beneath him and he had just enough of his senses left to cover his head as a deluge of rocks and stones came rattling down about them. He was deafened and his head rang like a bell. There was blood coming from his nose and ears. For a moment everything went black.

When he came round again he was conscious that his feet were hanging in space. He crawled forward and looked behind him. The edge of the cliff where they had been watching had gone. He couldn't make out very much of his surroundings because a dense pall of smoke concealed them from view.

'Jennings!' he called. 'Are you there?'

For what seemed a long time there was no reply and then he heard a faint answering call.

'Yeah. Leastways I think so.'

In spite of everything, Bendix couldn't help grinning. Coughing and wheezing, he struggled to sit upright. There was a hammer in his head beating out a loud insistent rhythm and he felt pain in various places where he had been hit by falling debris. Then, through the pall of smoke, he saw the figure of Jennings staggering towards him.

'That was a good idea to come up here,' he said.

'If we hadn't, we'd have met the full force of the blast,' Bendix replied.

Jennings helped Bendix to his feet and they both looked aghast at what had happened to the cliff where they had been lying. The crest of the mountain had been blown away and when they looked over the edge they saw huge piles of boulders lying among the trees below. Gilpin's burial mound was buried beneath rocks and shattered tree limbs. Where the cabin had stood was an empty, black, gaping space. Through the swirling smoke they could see burnt and blackened bodies of men and horses lying around what had been the yard; broken rags and remnants of flesh and limbs were scattered far and wide.

'Hell,' Jennings said. 'Somebody sure miscalculated. Nobody could have survived that.' He looked at Bendix through smoke begrimed eyes. 'I guess that's the end of the Presidio Kid.'

Bendix continued to survey the awful scene. Despite himself, he was looking for a black-clad figure in a long black mask.

'I guess so,' he said.

★　★　★

It was late at night and Bendix and Jennings were sitting together on the veranda of the marshal's house. They had both suffered cuts and bruises and

239

Bendix's head still hurt. The doctor had checked them over and pronounced that there was nothing serious. They had built smokes and their cigarettes glowed in the darkness.

'You know,' Jennings said, 'we never did get to find if anythin' was hidden in that cabin, and if so, just what it was.'

Bendix looked at the star-strewn sky and the moon, which was floating above the pale bell-like flowers of a Joshua tree.

'I used to think it was a hoard of money,' he said. 'Now I believe it was somethin' else.'

'Yeah? What was that?'

'Somethin' Miss Otilie waited a long time and came a long way to destroy.'

The marshal blew smoke from his mouth. 'I don't get you,' he said.

'I assumed Gilpin built that cabin as a means to escape, to be alone. Now I think he built it for him and the Presidio Kid to share. But he never came back. She waited and he never came back.'

'I still don't figure it,' the marshal

said. 'You say she was scarred up bad. Was that the reason he didn't return?'

'No, it wasn't the reason. I suppose she thought it was. But when Gilpin came out here and when he had finished building that cabin, he knew it was just a dream.'

'A dream? Seems like he went to a lot of trouble for nothin'.'

'Maybe so. But he knew better than anyone the person she was because, in his own way, he was in love with the Presidio Kid.'

The marshal stubbed out his cigarette. 'Perhaps you're right,' he said. 'But I still don't get it.'

'All the time she was runnin' the Rocking-Horse, she never really gave up on Gilpin. It was only when she knew for certain he wasn't ever coming back that she determined to destroy the last trace, the last symbol, of their love affair, and that was the cabin he had built.' Bendix lapsed into silence.

The marshal stood up and leaned against the veranda rail.

'I don't know,' he said. 'But even allowin' that they both had a bad attack of Cupid's cramp, I still figure Gilpin stashed the loot up there.'

Although the marshal could not see it in the dark, Bendix's face was wreathed in a gentle smile. First thing next morning he was riding for Horse Bend and the Eleven Half-Circle where Miranda Coolidge would be waiting.

THE END